P9-CNH-213

A12003 488117

FIC
MCI   McInerny, Ralph M.

              Still life.

$21.95   ONE WEEK

DATE			

NORMAL PUBLIC LIBRARY
NORMAL, ILLINOIS 61761

BAKER & TAYLOR

Still Life

Still Life

A Novel

Ralph McInerny

Five Star
Unity, Maine

NORMAL PUBLIC LIBRARY
NORMAL, ILLINOIS 61761

FIC
MCI

Copyright © 2000 by Ralph McInerny

All rights reserved.

This book is a work of fiction. Names, characters, places, and incidents are either products of the author's imagination or, if real, used fictitiously.

Five Star First Edition Mystery Series.

First Edition, Second Printing

Published in 2000 in conjunction with Tekno Books and Ed Gorman.

The text of this edition is unabridged.

Set in 11 pt. Plantin by Elena Picard.

Printed in the United States on permanent paper.

Library of Congress Cataloging-in-Publication Data

McInerny, Ralph M.
    Still life : a novel / Ralph McInerny.
        p. cm.—(Five Star first edition mystery series)
    ISBN 0-7862-2895-4 (hc : alk. paper)
    1. Police—Ohio—Fiction. 2. Missing persons—Fiction.
3. Ohio—Fiction. I. Title. II. Series.
PS3563.A31166 S75 2000
    813'.54—dc21   00-061724

A12003488117

To Tim Fuller
magister magistrorum

22.00   3/01

B&T

*"When a woman says that all men are animals
she is not referring to the tree of Porphyry."*
Rachel Salma

Part One

Manfredi

On CNN, a namesake of Manfredi's, no relation, though he couldn't prove it, was on trial in Palermo—a general in the Carabinieri wearing a uniform that would knock your eye out, a big guy, bald, huge silver mustache, and guilty as sin by the look of him. Manfredi had seen that look a million times in the course of growing old on the Fort Elbow, Ohio police force. He had walked a beat, he had risen to the rank of captain of detectives, finally he was put behind a desk and now, in the evening of his career, was in charge of special projects. A fancy title, a corner office, an assistant, and a secretary, but he was ending his career as a supernumerary, so why kid himself?

He was a freak and he knew it. For most cops, twenty years and a pension were all they could take. They went on to second jobs at malls and in banks, playing cop and being paid better than on the force. But Manfredi stayed on. His parents, scarred by the Depression in the Land of Plenty, had urged him to apply at the post office because no mailman ever lost his job during the Depression, but Manfredi took and passed the police exam and entered the police academy. His father was wary.

"No one shoots at a mailman, Egidio."

Thank God his father hadn't survived into a time when anyone might be a target of opportunity. Last week a grandmother had been shot while babysitting the neighbor's kids, a black lady with lovely manners who Manfredi treated with

9

unfeigned respect, proof that he wasn't a racist. The woman was apologetic for taking up so much of other people's time. The slug had grazed her skull.

"It did more damage to the window," she said. "Thank God the children were in bed."

Investigate and find out if someone had it in for the nice old lady and it wasn't random after all? Even if they had the resources for such inquiries, Manfredi would have nixed it. His opinion still had veto power anyway. He didn't want to know if some crazed, grizzled lover had taken a shot at the dignified Mrs. Fontaine. She had come to Fort Elbow from New Orleans thirty years before and raised a family that now disappointed her into the second and third generation. Digging into her life would be too much like digging into his own.

Why did he hang on? Next year, at 65, it would be all over whether he liked it or not, no arguments, the warm handshake, a ceremony, but still the bum's rush he had been postponing all these years. Maybe he should have called it quits at twenty years and settled in at the mall ogling young matrons. They'd had another complaint about Nealy, once one of Fort Elbow's finest, a little too helpful handing a woman into her car after he offered to help her with her groceries.

"Inadvertent," Nealy said, trying to act surprised at the accusation. "An inadvertent placement of the hand." That had worked the first two times but no more. *Retired Cop Cops Feel.* An item in Baxter's column, the bastard. He hated cops ever since he lost his driver's license for DUI.

Gloria, Manfredi's secretary, made it difficult for him to feel superior to Nealy. Female took on new meaning with Gloria. Manfredi had taken to shielding his eyes and watching her walk away through his fingers. He had shut Noonan up when he commented on Gloria's body. He didn't want his assistant to have any grounds for spreading rumors.

Noonan had taken the job as Manfredi's assistant to get out of uniform. He had thought riding in a patrol car was boring.

"What exactly is the job description?"

Manfredi told Noonan when his breaks came and how long he could take for lunch. He wasn't sure how serious a cop Noonan was. But if he was only a twenty-year man he would have welcomed nothing to do and a chance to look at Gloria while he did it. Since then they had gotten along. Still, Manfredi was the old bastard who liked to remember the way it used to be, and Noonan was young. Plus he had been to college.

"Ripeness is all," is what Noonan had said about Gloria when Manfredi told him to cool it.

"Manfredi, it's Shakespeare."

Noonan could be a pain in the ass in his own way but they got along. Maybe Noonan really wasn't just another twenty-year man.

Manfredi would be too old for a job at the mall when he retired, not that he would take it if offered. He had a hefty pension and with social security was all set. Teresa, a born worrier, didn't believe that, but then he didn't explain it to her either.

Lately he had even wondered, sometimes, if he could stand another year of active duty. The grandmother, Mrs. Fontaine, had been too much. The drugs were too much. The hustlers on Grand Avenue were too much. And there was more.

Now a professor wanted them to reopen an investigation into a murder committed thirty years ago. Noonan was all for it and Manfredi was wavering.

"We could at least check it out, Manfredi."

"What if the professor made it up?"

11

"Why the hell would a professor do that?"

"She's retired?"

"That's right."

"Old people are funny."

"I'm finding that out."

"Hey."

Ambrose

1

Ambrose Hennessy's eyes were good, except for distance, he had almost no aches or pains and he still had his hair. Only his hearing was gone, and he got no sympathy from anyone. He had asked Rachel to come to his room while he tested out the new digital hearing aids, both ears, with a control like a fountain pen that clipped into this shirt pocket. He held the control now, adjusting the sound with his thumb, turned away from Rachel.

"How can you hear me if you don't look at me?"

"Don't shout, Rachel. Speak in a normal voice."

"That's what I've been doing."

Irked, he swung toward her. He would never get used to her ridiculous red hair and the penciled brows. But a cruel remark died aborning. He had to test this goddam hearing aid and he needed a listener. He said patiently, "Do it again, Rachel."

Her lips moved and his thumb also moved, jamming the volume up as high as it would go. He could hear her voice but could not make out what she was saying.

"They want two thousand dollars for this thing."

"Save your money."

"For what?"

"For one that works. Or you might want to get married."

Hennessy ignored this. He had navigated into his eighth decade without the encumbrance of a wife, and he sure as hell wasn't going to weaken now. Not many women, or men, for

13

NORMAL PUBLIC LIBRARY
NORMAL, ILLINOIS 61761

that matter, aged gracefully, and God knew Rachel wasn't among them. Women who had been attractive in their middle years never really lost it. Alma, for example, with hair that might still be blond, bright blue eyes and rosy round cheeks, he could see her as a girl, yet she was probably as old as Rachel.

"Like Basil Bauer." She was shouting.

"This damned thing is no better than what I've got." He wouldn't buy it. Ears aren't like eyes, get the right lenses and you can see as well as before. Some nerve in the inner ear died and amplifying sound couldn't fix that.

"Did you see the invitation?" She stood next to him and lifted on her toes to speak right into his face. The cherry-colored lipstick gave her a clownish look. Invitation? Was she referring to her own coquettish manner? He ignored what she had said.

"Don't tell anyone about this, Rachel."

He didn't want a lot of gossip going around about his desperate effort to find the Fountain of Youth and hear like a dog. Whatever Rachel replied fell outside his auditory range. Those not affected by hearing loss had no idea how aggravating it was. For the deaf one. They knew well enough how irritating it was to be asked to repeat what they'd said. Ambrose had explained that to Basil—there are no outward signs of loss of hearing.

"Apart from your bewildered expression?" Wry, oblique, going more or less quietly into that dark night the poet said awaited them all, Basil was always perfectly audible to Ambrose. This could be explained; there were sounds he could pick up and others he could not. But this did not explain why certain voices lay in the proper register for him. That Basil's was one of them was an equivocal fact. If everyone spoke like Basil, Ambrose would never have realized he was going deaf. But already, years ago, he'd been asking people to speak up.

There were perhaps half a dozen former colleagues of Ambrose's living here at the Residenza, and Basil was one of them. They might have adjourned here for a final faculty meeting.

2

De Gaulle called old age a shipwreck—if Basil was correct in attributing the remark to the general—but Ambrose thought it was something anyone might have said, if not with the drama of the simile, still with the force of the meaning.

Item. Why did Rachel, a gifted and accomplished woman, try cosmetically to make herself look as she had at forty? Beauty had never been hers, not in her best years, but she supplied the want with desperate vanity, dying her hair and spreading makeup over her crumbling features. Yet Rachel knew the poetry of Pope and Dryden by the yard and was, as he told her, a bottomless source of Boswellian examples of Dr. Johnson's wit. "Hardly bottomless, Ambrose." The penciled brows rose suggestively above her frame-less glasses. She had half a dozen expensive pairs. Ambrose bought his at Osco Drugs, $9.95 a pair. "I will show you a picture of Johnson. And one of Boswell too for that matter." He amended his praise from a bottomless to a penetrating source. A mistake. "Have you any idea of the etymology of that word?" He looked it up, later, and was almost shocked. Does fascination with the flesh never flag? Surely, that sort of thing must have faded to a mere memory for Rachel now, and an illicit one at that.

Item. Why did Basil spend hours each day scanning into his computer the papers of a lifetime, preparatory to editing and arranging them? A final effort to make his professional career seem competitive with Lilian's? Or with Rachel's and Ambrose's, for that matter? How retirement made one naked to old academic enemies. Naked, period.

"Ambrose," Rachel said to him now, "you'll never guess who the bride to be is."

"That's an interesting combination—is and to be."

"Potency presupposes act." She tried to punch his arm, but he stepped aside. He was clipping the useless control to his shirt pocket.

"What bride?"

She made a disgusted, and disgusting, noise. "What have we been talking about?"

"One more fraudulent attempt to exploit the laudable desire of the hard of hearing to hear again."

"In the course of which the invitation came up."

"What invitation?"

"It is pinned to the bulletin board. Are your eyes going too?"

"Going? They've been. Invitation to what?"

"You know and you're teasing me." But she simpered rather than seethed. It was Rachel who was teasing him. Ye gods. Since he was through with her, Ambrose went to the door and opened it. Rachel remained where she had been, in full view of anyone walking by. She would need help getting up out of the chair into which she had collapsed. He went back and held out his hand. She gave him hers with feigned solemnity, but when he tugged on it she tugged back.

"Basil is getting married."

"Nonsense."

"That is the invitation. We are all asked to be there when a judge performs the ceremony."

"Basil is as old as I am."

16

"He is as *young* as you are."

"You're making up that invitation."

She settled more definitely into the chair. Ambrose looked at her and his mind was whirring. Was it possible that Basil Bauer would marry again at the age of seventy-two? He found that he could not dismiss the thought out of hand. He readied his desk chair to receive his descending bottom and sat. He stared at Rachel.

"Is it Alma?"

"Alma! Why would you think it's her?" Rachel spoke with quick, angry jealousy.

"It was all before your time."

"What was before my time?"

"It isn't Alma?"

"Certainly not." Rachel did want to rise now. His reaction had spoiled any pleasure she had hoped to derive from telling him the news. "And lest you think I have come to cushion the blow it doubtless is to you, it is not me either."

It would have been exaggeration to call the noise Ambrose then made a laugh, but it got Rachel to her feet. She careened toward the still open door and Ambrose rose and followed her.

"A younger woman?"

But Rachel ignored him. She put one hand on the doorframe before going into the corridor.

"Of course any woman would be younger," Ambrose said.

Just a look from the pinkish eyes.

"You're making it up, Rachel."

She said something he did not catch, and he was sure she had deliberately made it impossible for him to hear her. It was the final verdict on this supposed breakthrough for those suffering the tragedy of hearing loss. He closed the door and sat at his desk, easing the clipped remote control from his shirt pocket. The clip had little give to it and clung to the fabric like a tenacious cat. He assured himself that Basil would never marry again. But doubt began like a far off noise, not quite beyond the range of his inner ear.

3

Alma turned and her look was fresh as a baby's from the womb, in awe and wonder at the world, as if the world had not put her through her paces over the years. She had buried two husbands and seen her three children turn into moral midgets—her only son dispensed pornography from an Internet site, the server set up in the laundry room of his house until his wife found out and threw him and his electronic business out.

"She's had to go back to work, which is silly. Eddie is wallowing in money."

"Does she know this?" Ambrose asked.

"She calls it tainted, ill-gotten gains. And, of course, she's right."

Alma's eyes misted over. If only one of her own flesh and blood had shown such principled rectitude. The daughter-in-law had done what Alma herself would have done.

"Whose son is he?"

"Mine."

"I meant his father."

"Don't blame the father."

"It was just a question."

"Besides, his father was a saint."

She meant her first husband, Harold Twining, who had been Ambrose's colleague before he withered and died in his forties. Harold's disease, though rare in the general population, was common in the tribe from which he had taken an

eighth of his blood. It was money the state paid out to prov-
able descendants of the tribe, hounded from the area by white
settlers, that Eddie had used to set up his web site. Ah, the vagaries of justice.

"How are the girls?" They were the fruit of a second disas-
trous marriage.

"Don't ask."

"I already did."

"Do you even remember them?"

"I hardly remember Harold."

"Oh, don't say that."

"It's Basil I want to talk about."

Alma's silvery hair was worn in a pageboy and had a
bouncy vitality of its own. She said, "Rachel is furious."

"What do you think?"

"That Rachel had a crush on Basil herself."

"She has a crush on everyone."

"Ambrose, I believe you're bragging."

"We are all in our eighth decade, Alma. It is nonsense to
talk about marriage and crushes."

"Eighth decade! What an awful way to put it."

The more Ambrose thought about Basil getting married,
the more confused he became. Basil Bauer was the last
person he would have expected to freak out in old age.
Ambrose irrationally thought of what Basil was about to do as
the moral equivalent of Alma's porn-dealing son.

"Do you know the girl, Alma?"

"I've met her. I saw this coming."

"Why didn't you say something?"

"To you?"

"To his friends. Friends can't stand by while an old man
makes a fool of himself marrying some chickie-poo."

Alma seemed surprised by her own uncontrolled laughter.

19

"Chickie-poo!" And once more she exploded in laughter. "Ambrose, have you met her?"

He gathered that she was the girl with long hair, jeans and running shoes, who had been helping Basil computerize his papers. Alma proved to be a cornucopia of information. The girl's name was Virginia; she was thirty-four years old but still a graduate student, her studies having been delayed while she put her husband through medical school. Once established in his profession, he prescribed a placebo for himself and announced that he wanted a divorce.

"That's why she and Basil are getting married by a judge. The husband is alive and well."

For the first time Ambrose permitted himself to think of the religious objections to Basil's taking a wife. He could not marry her in the Church, and he would not consider marriage before a judge a real marriage.

"Harold was Catholic but I never became one," Alma said. "Haven't all those restrictions and regulations been swept away?"

"Was your Eddie raised Catholic?"

Alma looked at him as if he had made an accusation. Did he think that her son would not have gone into pornography if he had been given a Catholic upbringing? That put it rather simplistically, but to some such theory Ambrose would surely subscribe.

"Basil calls them neo-pagans."

"Basil?"

"He was speaking of his own children, but he might have been describing mine."

Lilian had borne Basil two children, a daughter and a son, and as far as Ambrose knew, they were nice enough people. Losing Lilian might have licensed them to fly off in any mindless direction, but they compensated for the loss of a parent by dedicating themselves passionately to the ordinary. To Success. Phyllis was a computer consultant, the source of Basil's impressive machine, while Gregory had made a career of money, his own and others, as a financial consultant. Basil had been scandalized by his children, particularly Gregory.

"People think the Church changed her mind on usury, Ambrose. As you well know, she did nothing of the kind. What Gregory does is worse than usury. Money is fruitful."

It was Basil's conceit that Ambrose was an authority on all religious matters. A conversation two weeks before on Basil's married status came back to him now as ominous, though at the time it had seemed a pointless discussion of canon law.

"In civil law Lilian has been dead for years."

"I don't think there is a provision in canon law for a lost spouse."

"She was never *lost*, Ambrose. She left me. Desertion is not a basis of annulment, of course, but civil law's judgment is that Lilian is dead. Canon law need only accept that."

Why had he imagined Basil was bringing it up after so many years? Masses could be said for Lilian, dead or alive. In canon law there was nothing comparable to insurance policies and retirement funds, but Basil had long since been deluged with money in compensation for the legally established death of Lilian. He had put the money in a special account, against her hoped-for return.

"Of course they'll want it back."

"Use the money, Basil."

"Never."

Money could never compensate for the loss of Lilian; Basil was right about that.

"How careful you've been, Ambrose."

Ambrose waited. Given the context, Basil might have been about to say anything.

"No hostages to fortune. No wife, no children. . . ."

But Basil did not sound remotely envious. He had lost his wife, a remarkable woman, and not in the most flattering way. She had left an enigmatic note. *"Basil. Forgive me, I am going. I want to be someone else. L."* Typed, unsigned, it had figured in stories of Lilian's disappearance. There were those who said Lilian had written it. Some said it had been Basil himself. Others thought it had been someone else. The note had provided the semblance of a reason for what was otherwise an unintelligible disappearance. Those who could imagine Lilian wanting no longer to be Mrs. Basil Bauer found it difficult to believe that she had wanted to cease being Lilian Dahl as well, but in ceasing to be the one she had ceased to be the other.

"Ambrose Bierce," Virginia had said. She had come first to Ambrose, seeking information on how best to approach the abandoned husband of the writer she idolized.

"B. Traven."

She smiled. "There must be others."

"Rimbaud in a way."

"Of course."

"And whatever happened to Waring? Browning."

"Browning disappeared?"

"No, no. Waring was a poetic character."

A fascinating theme, the artist who abandons his art at the height of his powers, but the mystery deepens when the artist vanishes into thin air as well. Ambrose disclaimed all knowledge of Lilian.

"But you were their best friend." She made it sound like an accusation. Perhaps it was.

"Basil and I were colleagues." He put back his head, closed his eyes, and tried to remember the lines from "The Ballad of Reading Gaol." Each man kills the thing he loves, ta da ta ta, ta da, the coward does it with a kiss, the brave man with a sword.

"Do you think that is what happened?"

"What?"

"That he killed her?"

"Have you talked with Basil yet?"

"I hoped that you would introduce me."

And he had, not even remotely thinking that he was thereby giving entree to Lilian's successor.

4

There had been a time in this country when a high school education was more demanding than many M.A. programs of the present era. Ambrose owned a Greek text of the *Iliad*, the first six books, Anthon's *Homer*, which had been in use in the New York public high schools in the 1890s. The slide had begun after World War II, when in an effort to do right by the boys who had beat the Germans and the Japs, the G.I. Bill was voted through by a congress only a minority of whose members had ever seen a college campus themselves, giving the veteran the right to government-paid education commensurate with his years of service. The G.I. Bill could be used to learn radio repair or take flying lessons or go to barber college, and in many instances was, but in the vast majority of cases it was a ticket to higher education and used accordingly. Since some veterans had spent four years in the service, they were eligible for enough support to go on to an advanced degree after receiving a bachelor's. But there was more. The veteran could take a G.E.D. test, a General Educational Development test, on the basis of which he was accorded credit and might begin his college education as a sophomore rather than freshman.

"What is the point of this pedantry, Ambrose?" But on that long-ago occasion, Basil might have been asking the question for Lilian's sake.

"I am explaining the origin of the institution to which we have devoted our lives."

"Go on." Basil sipped his bock beer. He could eat and drink at will and never gain a pound. For that matter he seemed never to get drunk. Ambrose Hennessy, on the other hand, was afloat on five beers which had loosened his tongue from all control.

"Please go on," Lilian added as if to compensate for the mere tolerance in her husband's voice. "Whenever you reminisce, I feel I understand you both better."

But it was himself he spoke for, not Basil, nor in this stage of lubrication did he repress the sublimated lubricity the sight of Lilian elicited, her legs curled up beside her on the couch, her hair plaited in a massive braid which lay upon her shoulder where she could caress it while she listened. Hennessy was assailed by thoughts of the barmaids in *Ulysses* gripping the beer pulls. Shame on him.

"Nor can we forget the 52/20 Club."

"I want to know everything," Lilian said, and as a poet of course she did. She was a filter through which everything must pass if any poetry was to emerge from her.

" 'Soft sift in an hour glass,' " he had said, and he was almost disappointed that the phrase was Hopkins', not hers.

"I had forgotten that, Ambrose," Basil said, not referring to Hopkins.

For upward of 52 weeks the returned and unemployed veteran was eligible for twenty dollars a week, payable at the local unemployment bureau on statement that he was not working nor was the kind of work he did available. In Minneapolis, they were advised to give deep sea diving as their line of work. Everyone was in collusion to help the returning heroes. Ambrose Hennessy had fought his war on land, in California, assigned to Camp Miramar where other units and even individual Marines spent shorter or longer periods before reassignment. His own assignment was temporary. Eventually he too would go into battle in the Pacific, that was the idea, but meanwhile duty at Miramar was almost sybaritic, whether for those just passing through or, for eighteen months, Ambrose Hennessy, PFC, USMCR. When he wasn't feeling remorse for it, confessing and attending a weekday as well as Sunday Mass in reparation, he took liberty in Tijuana in every sense of the term. Hennessy had tasted the effects of marijuana two decades before the rage, by which time he had become a stern and disapproving moralist in the matter. And he had sinned in the cribs of two-dollar whores. It was incredible that one could simply wait in line to have a girl who, however quick she was about it, would do anything he wanted. The line to get into confession bore an unsettling resemblance to that south of the border, an analogy he confessed as a sacrilegious thought.

"It sounded like a night club." Lilian meant 52/20.

Basil told Lilian that you could spend the twenty dollars where you liked. They marveled at what twenty dollars had meant in those days.

"I was paid seventy-five a month in the Marines."

Basil had been a sergeant, but in the army, which apart from more pay meant nothing. Ambrose had been scandalized by how easy promotions came in the army, and in the navy too, but the navy had been an enemy force in his boot-camp-trained mind. Swabbies were despised, not least for being taught that marines were sea-going bellhops. Twenty dollars a week had supported Hennessy through a summer at the main beach at Lake Nokomis and nights in the bars of Mendota. He entered the University of Minnesota that fall, as a sophomore, major English, ambition to be a writer. Two years later, coming out of a writing class in Folwell Hall, he stopped to study the names of the faculty on a door across the hall. One caught his eye, not only because it was vaguely familiar, but because he had read *The Dangling Man*. Saul Bellow.

Basil was studying history, enthralled by the gassy lectures of Professor Deutsch, which concerned the European war in which Basil had fought. Basil's combat experience, however modest, was a touchy subject. In his heart of hearts, Ambrose did not believe that even combat made an army sergeant equal to a marine PFC. It was Ambrose who first met Lilian, in a writing class, she a freshman, he a senior, and then had made the epochal mistake of introducing her to Basil.

carried about inside a cage,
my heart, dear heart, was free,
swinging slowly on its perch
it took delight to see
the prisoners outside in search
of entrance to my cage . . .

Those were the lines with which Lilian began the poem commemorating the day Ambrose introduced her to Basil in the Union. They remained a trio of sorts, but Ambrose had been reduced to the role of chaperone, duenna. He tried to convince them that a similar situation had prompted Rilke to write the famous elegies.

"You were explaining the origin of this campus."

For an historian Basil was remarkably uncurious about his own historical situation. The flood of veterans into colleges and universities had the dual effect of making it seem normal

26

to attend college, which had not been the case hitherto, and because of it increased the need for faculty. The Minneapolis campus ballooned to an enrollment of thirty thousand and the campus at Duluth, begun as a two-year feeder for the main campus, soon became a four-year campus, conferring degrees of its own. It was a harbinger of the many campuses of the University of Minnesota that would eventually be founded in their native state. But Ambrose, content with a master's, had been hired at the newly established branch of the University of Ohio at Fort Elbow, what had once been a normal college expanding accordingly. In those informal days, Ambrose alerted Basil to the opening in history and the Bauers came to Fort Elbow; there were writing courses for Lilian to teach. After a hiatus of a year and a half, the trio was once again together.

When Ambrose met Virginia he had the eerie sense that she was Lilian rediviva, but her deference was more for the disappeared poet than for the professor emeritus whose papers she had agreed to computerize. Ambrose said that was a word he despised.

"No, Ambrose," Basil said. "It is the computer you despise."

"I feel toward the computer what I feel toward the fountain pen. It is an instrument."

Virginia followed their conversation as if it was a tennis match, though a game consisting mainly of lobs. She asked Ambrose if he had a computer.

"Of course." He took out a pencil and tapped his head.

Virginia laughed. Ambrose liked this young woman with her tragic past. Lilian would have liked her too.

"Do *you* have any of Lilian's papers?"

Ambrose was startled by the question.

"Letters, for instance?"

"Why would she write letters to me? We saw one another almost daily. You write letters to absent people."

"Did she write anyone after she left?"

Basil moaned, but he was loving all this attention. "The police were equally persistent."

"Of course, the police would have investigated."

"A lot of good that did."

"I'll see what they have." She made a little note.

"You shouldn't encourage her to dig into all that, Basil."

"I couldn't stop her if I wanted to."

"And you don't want to."

"She is such a sympathetic soul."

Coeds as a rule got a crush on Basil. He was less impressive to male students, but then he had become ethereal over the years, developing into his imagined version of the legendary Professor Deutsch. He was equally successful as a lecturer, but of course Fort Elbow was a smaller pond.

Virginia brought organization and efficiency to Basil's project. As she had hoped, his file cabinets and cardboard boxes were full of Lilian's things. There had been a time when Ambrose had longed to go through her papers. Once he suggested to Basil that they owed it to Lilian to sort out her things.

"There could be a posthumous volume."

"She isn't dead."

Did he think repeating that would make it so? You would have thought he'd prefer a wife safely dead than one still wandering the world, her freedom a rebuke to their marriage. Her disillusion was everywhere in the poems, for one who had eyes to see.

word and gesture
were soul to soul once

even cor ad cor—
will we ever attain
the twain again
that marked us once before . . .

"He says it is his favorite," Virginia said to Ambrose.
"He has a tin ear for poetry."
"It's so sad."
"O la vie est triste, trop triste, incurablement triste . . ."
"I can see why Lilian got along with you."
"She was a joy to be with. They both were."
"What do you think happened?"
"Whatever happened, she is dead."
Virginia shook her head slowly. "A human body is pretty hard to overlook. Wouldn't she have been found?"

Ambrose told her of cars discovered in the spring when the last ice had gone, and small aircraft could spot them at the bottom of the river. Invariably it was someone who had been reported missing. They were thought to have simply gone away. But what had happened was that their car had gone into the river, jumped a curb, spun out on ice. Within minutes the driver would be dead, but months passed before this was known. In the meantime it was permitted to hope that the missing person would return alive.

"You think she's in the river?"
"I was responding to your remark that it is hard to overlook a human body. Sometimes it's hard to do anything else."
"There is at least one more collection of her poems. It has to be published."
"What does Basil say?"
"Would you talk to him?"

Manfredi

When Noonan continued to bring up the matter of Mrs. Fontaine, the black grandmother who had been the near-victim of a drive-by shooting, Manfredi diverted him by professing to have second thoughts about the thirty-year-old murder the professor had called in about. It turned out that the professor was a woman, and Noonan had taken a course from her.

"Restoration comedy."

"What's that?"

"I still have the notes I took."

"What's restoration comedy?" Manfredi repeated.

Noonan scraped his bristled chin with the credit card he claimed he could open locks with. "You know what restoration means, don't you?"

"Try me."

"Someone buys an old car and makes it good as new? We say he restored it."

"Where's the comedy, Noonan?"

"My trying to teach you something. You want to hear what Rachel Salma had to say?"

"You still have your notes?"

"Funny."

"As in comedy?"

It was their way of getting along, harassing one another. Gloria got on edge when they got going, ready to reconcile all differences.

"He wants to pry into the life of Mrs. Grace Fontaine."

Gloria frowned. "That woman needs protection."

"Would keeping her out of the paper help or hurt her?"

Gloria thought again. "Better leave it where it lays."

"That's why Noonan has been out sweet-talking one of his lady professors."

"She professes to be a lady?"

"Do you do restoration comedy?"

The way Noonan spoke of Professor Salma, she could use a little reconstruction herself. The first impression, that she was at most middle-aged, went fast when you took a close look.

"Why would a woman dye her hair, Gloria?" Noonan seemed genuinely perplexed.

"Now you just hush, young man. You don't know anything about it."

Maybe Noonan thought Gloria's frosted hair was natural. He became all business and read his report. Gloria stopped what she was doing and listened to Noonan's account of the disappearance thirty years before of a poet married to a member of the local branch of the state university. As he spoke, Gloria brought up on the computer the record of the investigation.

Lilian Dahl, Mrs. Basil Bauer, 39, had been declared a missing person after a brief investigation following a phone call from her husband. Bauer said he was not really worried. His wife was an artist and apt to act in a way that others might regard as impulsive. He was sure she had felt a need to be by herself and simply acted. So why had he bothered to call the police? At the urging of friends, actually. He had named two other members of the faculty, Professor Ambrose Hennessy and Professor Rachel Salma, both in English, both close to the man and his missing wife. Their interviews were in

31

marked contrast with Bauer's.

Rachel thought there must be another man, not that she had any definite suspects, but a woman just knows these things. Whoever talked with her had let her run on and then written a long report, but whatever it had sounded like thirty years ago, it now read like groundless speculation.

"And she's the one who wants you looking into it again?" The corners of Gloria's mouth went down and she turned her head to look at Noonan from the corner of her eye.

"Listen to what Ambrose Hennessy said."

Hennessy had thought Mrs. Bauer might be dead, not just missing. The Bauers were a strange couple, oil and water. Bauer taught history and had a narrow and literal mind, whereas his wife had won national acclaim as a poet. He wondered if the interviewer would like to hear how Kierkegaard had talked of the poet. The interviewer suggested some other time. Hennessy got rather short shrift.

"That man is jealous," Gloria said.

"He still alive?"

"You want me to find out?"

"Just take his pulse, okay. I'm not giving you carte blanche."

"Watch it," Gloria said.

Basil

1

"I'm not going to tell you what to do, Dad." Phyllis looked like neither Lilian nor himself, although Lilian had professed to see strains of her father's family in Phyllis. She had a cousin whom Phyllis resembled. The way they talked about her suggested that they had doubts about her origin. Phyllis had weighed nearly 15 pounds at birth and was nearly as tall as Lilian when she was thirteen; not that Lilian was all that tall, but that proved to be the end of it anyway. Before she stopped growing, Phyllis had developed the stooped posture of the tall and her homely face wore a benign expression. "Will you stay here?"

Both his children felt the mandatory shame at having a parent in a nursing home. Actually, Basil had never lived better. He didn't have to worry about meals, or go out for them, and his room was kept spotless. The office he had rented near the mall had come to look like his old faculty office. It was largely there that his surprising romance with Virginia had bloomed.

"Can you afford it?" Gregory wanted to know.

"She has a graduate fellowship. I suppose she will get a teaching position."

"So what do you have, social security, your pension?"

"I'm fine."

"You never had much of a portfolio, did you?"

"Should I have?"

Gregory smiled. "People invest with an eye to reaching the

33

age you are. Did you talk with someone at the college when you retired?"

What a stranger he seemed to be to his son. Basil had no idea what Gregory would make of his assets if they did discuss them, something Gregory was obviously reluctant to do. He spent all day talking about money; this visit to Fort Elbow must be respite from that. Still, he looked around with a cold eye.

"To think I am preparing people for places like this."

"Most of us are quite content here."

"Good. Good. What's she like?"

"Young."

Gregory looked at him steadily, mentally rejecting things he would not say. "How's your health?"

"What an odd question."

But Gregory had some stories he wished to tell his father. In Miami old men died of sexual excitement in porn parlors. They married much younger women and killed themselves trying to please them. It was a well-known medical fact that the male body was not up to the same things in seniors as in younger men.

"Forget that old line about dying with a smile on your face. Usually it's cardiac arrest."

Basil could not remember ever talking to his son about such things before. He was surprised to find Gregory so knowledgeable, but then he had probably done a little research in preparation for this visit. Basil said he would try not to lose his head.

"I get to Chicago now and then, the airport, downtown, but I haven't seen the Midwest for years." This had the force of a negative judgment. The heart of the country had let Gregory down just as he was warning Basil his own could. "You don't want me back for the ceremony, do you?"

"Good heavens no. It will be a simple pagan rite in the recreation room."

"Phyllis tells me you've found an apartment."

"Near campus."

Gregory nodded. Were no childhood memories stirred? Could he recall Lilian at all? Basil had provided both Phyllis and Gregory with an album of photographs of the family they had once been, father, mother, children. He had included the poems Lilian had written for each of her children, none of which had been published.

"I always liked this one," Phyllis had said, meaning she was no student of her mother's writing. He had never shown them these poems before.

Gregory moved his lips as his read his mother's lines written when he was one year old. He began to nod before he lifted his eyes to his father. He turned his head once to the side, returned it to his regular position and that was that.

Basil did not condemn them for this. Obviously they had inherited his own limited response to poetry and were not attracted to Lilian's bardic swath through life.

Virginia, on the other hand, seemed to have most of Lilian's published work memorized. Basil had found this unsettling at first, as if he were being quizzed, but Virginia seemed to think he was reticent about displaying his emotions when it came to Lilian and her writing. She made him realize what a career of sorts he had made of being the husband of the writer who had simply disappeared. *"Basil. Forgive me, I am going. I want to be someone else. L."* Her note, remembered, could always sting tears from his eyes if only because it brought back the thought that he had been left holding the bag, he would have to raise the kids, Lilian had flown free of all that.

2

"Knowing you seems to bring me closer to her," Virginia said.

Basil put his hand over Virginia's. Hearing her read Lilian's words was like having his wife back again at last, as he had always insisted she would be. Going off as she had was the sort of thing that poets do, everyone knew that, it had nothing to do with irresponsibility in the usual sense or falling out of love.

"I think of her continuing to write during all these years."

"Oh, I am sure she did."

"Those poems will explain her action."

"It doesn't need any explanation."

Virginia always took Lilian's side, that had been plain from the outset, and Basil edited what he said accordingly. As soon as she told him about herself, during the interview, he suspected what her real interest was, though at the time she insisted that helping him computerize his papers was exactly the kind of work she was looking for.

"A change of pace."

"Of course."

"I don't have to tell you about the life of a graduate student."

But she would have had to, if he were interested. Ten years away from the campus had made him a total stranger there. None of his memories seemed to match what the place had become. To Ambrose Hennessy he voiced the opinion that they had gotten out just in time.

"It was always crazy. You should have kept a link."

Ambrose shared a campus office with two other emeriti. He used it less often than he claimed, but still he need not feel

36

like an intruder walking those old walks. And he could use the library. Virginia had in effect renewed Basil's ties with the campus and of course she had library privileges and could bring him books.

"I wrote only the one book, the monograph on Rasputin. Could a rascal be a good ruler? That was the question, not the title."

"What is the answer?"

"Russia would have been worse without the influence of Rasputin."

"You read Russian?"

"They gave me a crash course in the army. I was always good at languages. Lilian envied that. We talked of doing some translations together. I would put things into English, she would put them into poetry."

"How did she write?"

She meant where, when, with what, how much. Had Lilian sat brooding like a poet in a movie, Omar Sharif writing the Lara poems, and then neatly putting them on paper? Virginia was shocked when he told her Lilian had worked on the typewriter.

"To transcribe, you mean?"

"No. To compose. You've seen her handwriting. She said that writing poetry is half typography. She had to see how a line would look printed."

"She would have liked the computer."

"Maybe not. She wouldn't have an electric typewriter. That's her machine."

Virginia rose and moved toward the old L. C. Smith on the shelf behind Basil's desk as the high priest had approached the Holy of Holies, as the pious approach the shrine at Lourdes, as Rachel had gone through Dr. Johnson's London house. When Virginia touched the old machine you would have thought she was hoping for a cure.

"Where will we work?"

"Why not here?"

"Of course."

But her tone brought back the way women persuade. She conveyed to him without saying it that she thought it was a bad idea to think they could work on his papers in his room. He began to mention the limitations of working here and she dismissed them all. He took the bait gladly, an old dog learning his old tricks again. It became established that he was the one who found his room a poor place in which to work, while she was its defender.

"Of course if you do insist on looking into alternatives . . . ."

"Ambrose Hennessy has an office on campus. He has to share it with other emeriti."

"Oh, you have to have privacy."

Virginia knew of offices for rent near the mall. The buildings embodied every current architectural cliché and surrounded an artificial pond. He rented a suite, and Virginia had his computer and file cabinets and boxes of books moved there. She bought a scanner at Best Buy and had it installed. Also a laser printer.

"Solomon in all his glory was not arrayed as one of these."

"Solomon?"

"I thought you were Catholic."

"Only on my father's side."

"I had a mole on my mother's side." Basil burst out laughing, remembering Lilian bursting out laughing when Ambrose had quoted that old Vaudeville line. Virginia was a good sport about this private joke. Told of Lilian's reaction, she laughed too.

Was it sick to imagine that Virginia was Lilian? This could

have been easily managed in a B movie with cryonics, put a
woman in a freezer to stop the aging process and thaw her out
later, a Rip Van Winkle without the nuisance of a beard. Virginia was more or less Lilian's age when she left. In his heart
of hearts, he decided she was Lilian, which meant she was already his wife and the little ceremony before the judge meant
nothing. Not that he could explain it to Monsignor Kelly.

"She's already got a husband, Basil."

"I could be said to already have a wife."

"What's the point, anyway?"

Monsignor Kelly was ten years older than Basil, still active
in pastoral work, though his status was assistant not pastor.
("They can make me a goddam altar boy so long as I can keep
working." Kelly's swearing no longer bothered Basil. The
priest claimed he had picked it up working on a state highway
crew summers as a seminarian. When he was put under for
his prostate operation he expected the worst. "They said I
spoke Latin all the time, or sang it. Me, singing?") It had been
silly to think Kelly would wink and look the other way in the
matter of Basil's marriage.

"Basil, you're a practicing Catholic."

"It's largely a matter of habit."

"What's wrong with that. Virtues are habits."

"But are habits virtues?"

"Bah."

Basil was inclined to agree. On the other hand, he was now
determined to marry Virginia. If she was a youthful Lilian she
reminded him of his younger self before they had begun to
practice what Lilian had called the Trappist method of birth
control. Total abstinence. They had two children, they could
not afford more, neither of them was inclined to try methods
involving temperatures and charts. Taking a vacation from all
that had been Basil's idea.

"You think you can do that?"

"Don't worry about me."

"Okay. Can we worry about me?"

Basil chuckled. He belonged to the school that held that women simulate sexual desire as a way of attracting and holding a man. It is the ticket to marriage and children to nurse and cherish, but the deed itself? Come on. For a woman it must be like losing a wrestling match.

"Basil," Lilian laughed. "You've actually turned a phrase."

Her laughter seemed to put the seal upon it. He got a hide-a-bed couch for the study and after a chaste kiss goodnight slipped away to solitude. It hadn't been bad at all. It became a habit if not a virtue. Later, of course, he wondered if that decision had played any part in Lilian's departure.

Virginia brought back memories of how nice it had been prior to that decision, snug in their double bed spooned up against Lilian, his hand on her breast, his face in her hair. Sometimes this led on to something more, sometimes not, but they had always been one flesh, not two. Had he thought they could still be as one with him on his pullout bed in the study and Lilian all alone in the bower that had been theirs?

After Lilian left he went on sleeping in the study, but he had resolved that when she returned it would be back to the double bed for the two of them for good.

3

"I'm surprised you're surprised, Ambrose. I should have thought you would see it coming."

"Friends are to keep us from making asses of ourselves, Basil."

"How can I prevent you from doing just that? I assure you

that I have considered this from every conceivable angle."

"Including the fact that you will be excommunicating yourself by contracting a marriage with someone already married."

"Is that true?"

"Ask Monsignor Kelly."

"I have discussed this with him."

"Don't tell me he gave you his blessing."

"All right."

Ambrose began to make a kind of humming noise. He seemed unaware that he did this. Perhaps he could not himself hear it. A question suddenly formed itself.

"Ambrose, tell me something."

"Ask."

"Does a deaf person have the same trouble hearing himself as he does other people?"

Ambrose glared at him. "Well, if we're going to be that personal, let me ask you something. I could understand if you had decided to marry someone like Rachel. She would be a good companion; you have a lot in common. I suppose she would be content with a little squeeze now and again. But a young woman will have expectations of a more ardent sort. Basil, do you think you can still perform?"

"I know I can."

"You do."

"Your question had occurred to me earlier. The only way of answering was to put myself to the test."

Ambrose was too embarrassed and angry to pursue it. Basil had counted on that. It doubtless was ungallant to suggest that Virginia had already given herself to him. But they had touched on such matters.

"Virginia isn't just my name, Basil. It's my condition."

"But you've been married. You have children."

41

"By artificial insemination. My husband could not perform the act himself. Our child was conceived of his sperm and my egg in a petri dish in the lab. Then it was implanted in me."

"A maculate conception."

"You disapprove."

"Ambrose could tell you of the Church document that condemns artificial insemination, surrogate parenthood, the lot."

"It was no real solution for us."

"But you did have a baby?"

"A manufactured baby. Unfortunately he died."

At the time, she wondered if there would be lasting effects of being conceived in that way. That had been a vast unknown when the procedure began.

"I read Huxley's *Brave New World* for the first time after Wallace was born. If I had read it before I would never have done what we did."

"We won't have children, okay?"

She laughed and kissed him, and he put his arm possessively about her waist and lay his cheek on her bosom. When she spoke he felt like a human stethoscope. He pulled back.

"I must suggest that to Ambrose."

"Having a baby?"

"Using a stethoscope as a hearing aid. Why would you think I'd tell him to have a baby?"

She brought his head back against her breast. "I was saying that it could probably be done with your seed and my egg, the way I did it before."

"I couldn't do it in front of strangers."

She started to explain the process but he stopped her. He had enough trouble with Monsignor Kelly without producing a test tube baby.

Basil asked Ambrose if he didn't find a resemblance between Virginia and Lilian.

"Basil, I have reached the age when any two people seem to have things in common."

"I have yet to reach that age. You're just being perverse."

"Perverse? Am I the one who wants to hold the body of a mere child in my arms, try the task of lover?"

"I believe you're fearful I may succeed."

"You'll succeed in making that woman a widow in pretty short order. How long do you think you'll live?"

"I'll live a lot longer living than by pretending I'm already dead."

"You read that somewhere."

"I think I'll write it down so I can read it to Virginia."

Ambrose looked around the room with a scowl. It seemed bare with most of the books gone and the computer removed as well as the file cabinets. Ambrose resented Basil's new office at the mall.

"Why do you need an office at all? Once everything is on the computer, you can turn the papers over to the archives. The whole thing will be on disks and you could work on those with a laptop computer."

"I feel I've already given them away."

"They could have remained right here as long as you did."

A new office, a new apartment, a new wife. Ambrose might feel resentment, but Basil felt excitement. Or so he told Virginia and himself. His children applauded the move. Get a load of dad. They had met Virginia and sounded a bit as if they were interviewing a nurse, condescending to him, straightforward with her. Why the hell didn't they have some resentment, anyway? For that he had Hennessy, and he was almost glad.

"It's been lonely, Ambrose."

43

Hennessy nodded, disarmed by the change of tone. That was the thing, make an ally of Ambrose. He did not want to lose his friendship. Virginia liked him, which was more than she could honestly say about Rachel.

"Here is a fantasy, Ambrose. Right out of *Wuthering Heights*. We're gathered in the recreation room, the judge is under way when the doors burst open and there is Lilian at last, stopping me from entering a bigamous marriage."

"She's dead, Basil."

Three words that seemed to fall from a great height, one by one. Ambrose wore a solemn expression.

"You talk as if you'd found her body."

"She's dead, Basil."

4

"I hate loose ends, Basil."

"Rachel, it was thoroughly investigated at the time. I am finally dropping my romantic pretense that she is still alive and will one day walk into the room as if she had just gone off to the store."

"Hawthorne."

"I don't understand."

"One of the tales. A man deserts his family but takes up residence a block away."

"Ambrose is certain she is dead. He has been all along."

"Where would he get such certainty?"

"That's odd. Poor Ambrose. I think he was under some kind of suspicion at the time of the original inquiry."

"How thorough an inquiry was it?"

"I begged them to stop it. They just talked to a lot of people and managed to stir up all kinds of rumors and theories."

"Didn't they talk with you?"

"Endlessly. For all the good it did."

"Basil, it isn't too late to have a true investigation now."

"It's been thirty years."

"And people are older. They have nothing to lose. Old people are more honest, Basil."

"I hadn't noticed."

Manfredi

1

Self-taught on the matter through the *National Geographic Magazine*, before the society hit television and brought animal pornography to the viewer, Manfredi likened the investigation he had reluctantly revived into the death of Lilian Dahl a.k.a. Mrs. Basil Bauer to an archeological dig.

The house, first of all. There it stood, the address as it appeared in all the accounts, a two-story brick on Collier Avenue, within walking distance of the campus. Once the street had been lined by elms, but most of them were gone now. That was why the house looked misplaced. It had been designed to be seen from a distance through surrounding trees.

"Thirty-four."

"Thirty-four what?"

"Trees," he explained to Noonan. "One of our predecessors actually counted the number of trees on this lot."

"Then he couldn't count." Two large pines in front, the magnolia on the east side and in back a dogwood.

"Wrong. They've been taken down. They weren't all Dutch elms. Why?"

"Can we go talk to some survivors now, before they die?"

"We haven't looked at the house yet. Noonan, this is where she was last seen."

Manfredi had spotted the For Sale sign in front of the house with the add-on indicating that there would be an open house on Sunday. Now he made Noonan feel good by saying they could keep the appointment with Rachel Salma. Manfredi had decided to go through the house on Sunday when he saw the name of the real estate agent on the sign. Marian Casey was the wife of a cop.

Twenty minutes later, Noonan pulled under the overhang of the retirement home and a woman in a cape-like coat, her arms emerging from slits, wearing opaque sunglasses, with red hair that looked like a fright wig, stepped out of the shadows and stooped to peer at the car.

"That's her." His eagerness was under control. The woman had insisted on being taken off the premises. Noonan had thought that significant, even after thirty years. In person, Professor emerita Salma seemed the very soul of caution. Noonan got out and opened the back door for her, and she entered on a cloud of perfume. Her tobacco-scented sigh was theatrical. "Thank you."

Noonan got back behind the wheel and the car began to roll. Before Manfredi turned away, the woman took off the sunglasses and gave him the full benefit of her eye makeup.

"I, needless to say, am Rachel Salma."

She reached for him and Manfredi had the crazy thought that she was going to test him for plumpness. He ignored the hand, nodded and told her who he was.

"So you are the redoubtable Manfredi."

"The captain and I took a look at the house on the way here."

"The house."

"Where Lilian Bauer lived."

She fell back, stirring up another cloud of perfume. "I want to weep when I think of that neighborhood."

"I suppose you remember tree-lined streets."

"The trees are only a symbol. I remember when it was safe for a woman to walk those streets. Faculty were heavily repre-

47

sented, of course, but there were other professionals. The school, Louis Agassiz, rivaled private schools in placing its graduates in college. Like all the others, it is now a monument to illiteracy."

"Blacks moved in?" Manfredi asked.

"It is not a matter of race. There were two black families way back then, and an oriental."

In the mall there was a Chinese restaurant that operated on the smorgasbord principle. All you could eat for $9.95. Going there had been a condition of Professor Salma's cooperation. She loaded up; her haughty gourmet's appraisal of the items contrasting with the gusto with which she heaped her plate.

"We can go through again." She seemed to be reassuring herself.

Manfredi took a bowl of won ton and some shrimp fried rice. Since this was in the line of duty, Noonan rivaled the professor in the quantity and variety of his selection. The green square tables had red paper coverings, green paper napkins, a bottle of soy sauce and another of hot mustard.

"You should see this place at night." Having accounted for the fact that they were the only ones there, the professor fell to. Age had not affected her appetite and for some minutes there was no question of talking. Noonan won what seemed a contest to empty one's plate first and freshened her tea.

"What is the first thing you think needs looking into?"

She shook her head and nodded toward the food line. There was still eating to be done before she was ready to explain her insistence that the inquiry into Lilian Bauer's disappearance be reopened.

"The first thing to know is that she was never known as Lilian Bauer. It was unheard of then, but she retained her maiden name. Dale. It was by that name that she was known and had been known before marrying Basil Bauer." She leaned toward Manfredi. The beads around her neck were large as marbles. "She was every woman's rival."

Her tongue loosened by oriental delicacies, Rachel Salma proved to be a storehouse of useless information. It was clear to Manfredi that her interest was to be the center of attention, and that she was at the green square table in the Empress of Hong Kong, two men listening attentively to her every word. Noonan's interest seemed unfeigned, but then he had felt under-worked for weeks. Rachel Salma served for him the valuable function of giving his professional life new meaning. He in turn was a susceptible male. Manfredi decided to leave the two of them alone. The soup had tasted like an emetic and the fried rice might have been left over from yesterday.

"Oh," Rachel said when he rose. Her lipstick had not been repaired since her assault on the food and this took away from her pout.

"I will hear everything from Detective Noonan."

"Of course."

"You can take credit for bringing us into it again, after all these years."

He regretted throwing her this bone. She was getting all the reassurance she needed from Noonan. She had been looking the younger man over, as if, having assuaged one appetite, she was ready to cater to another.

2

On Sunday he arrived unannounced at the open house on Collier Avenue. There was one car in the driveway and that was it. It proved to be Marian Casey's. She seemed both glad and disappointed to see him.

"Or are you interested in the house?"

"In a manner of speaking."

Marian had taken on the Collier house as a personal challenge. It was in the modified prairie style, had been kept in good repair and was worth far more than it would get, given what had happened to the neighborhood.

"I'd like to see a young family in here. It's a family house."

"How's the school?"

"A family who'd send their kids to private school. Oh, it couldn't be just anyone. They'd have to see the merits of the house. They would have to be willing to take a few social risks. Not everyone has to live in the suburbs!"

Marian was a handsome woman, with a helmet of black hair that swished around with every movement of her head then fell back into perfect shape. Olive skin, large expressive eyes, in love with her work which was as demanding as her husband's. Imagine spending Sunday afternoons like this, and during the week she would have to be on call evenings when clients were free to look at houses. She was very good at what she did. Manfredi took the tour of the house with her, and while he did he imagined the house as it had been thirty years ago.

"Have there been a lot of owners?"

Marian, of course, had such information at her fingertips. Built in 1913, the house had been occupied by the original owner until 1929. Through the Depression it had changed hands four times, to the benefit of the banks involved, but during World War II it had been bought by a local architect who had tried to conduct his business from it, apparently running afoul of various zoning statutes. He had been captivated by the design of the house, but he sold it in 1951.

"To Basil Bauer."

"That's right!"

"Do you realize that Lilian Dahl the poet lived here?"

"Tell me about it."

He gave her a quick account and told her what his interest in the house was. A couple arrived then and while Marian showed them around, Manfredi took another tour of the house. A room at the back of the first floor must have been the study. It looked out on the very large backyard. The walls were lined with bookshelves, empty, "than which there is no sadder sight." The phrase was from Rachel, describing Basil Bauer's room at the retirement home now that he had rented an office. Empty houses are harder to sell, Marian had told him. Manfredi did not have the imagination to furnish this one. In the basement there was a workbench that looked as if it had been there long enough to be the one Lilian had used when she tried to branch out into papier-mâché art. When he came upstairs, he stopped to listen to Marian.

"Have you heard of a poet named Lilian Dahl?"

"Oh yes," the woman said.

"This was her house."

"It was! Of course I knew she lived in Fort Elbow, but . . . Honey, think of it. Lilian Dahl."

She went on in an altered voice. Apparently she was reciting. Manfredi just waved as he left, not wanting to disturb Marian. She called him that night.

"They're going to make an offer. It was the poet who did it. Why do you know about her?"

"Her husband reported her as a missing person."

"She's still alive?"

"He prefers to think so."

"Aw."

3

He went out to the house on Collier again, having gotten a key from a grateful Marian Casey. The exploring he had been able to do alone on Sunday after the now prospective new owners appeared had whetted his appetite to spend more time there, to conjure of the *genius loci,* as Rachel Salma had put it.

"But the genius of the place has fled."

"That isn't what it means."

There is something in the professorial voice that warns the alert listener that a lecture is about to begin. Manfredi tuned her out. She had become for him a comical personage, and it seemed a commentary on his decaying judgment that he had permitted her importuning to unleash Noonan on a matter that must have been resolved one way or another decades ago. But he himself was caught up in the matter now, as witness his secret visit to the Collier house, in the unexpressed hope that he might steal a march on Noonan. He had, after all, been pretty good in his time.

The house, though unfurnished, was not empty, not when one thought of the reason for this visit. Where things happen has a permanence denied the agents of those happenings. This house, these walls, these rooms, enjoyed a species of immortality. How many who had lived here were now dead?

Upstairs in the master bedroom he stood and thought unseemly thoughts of the intimacies of others. There was a special poignancy in the passion of a woman who had disappeared thirty years ago. What was the phrase Brother Albert had repeated in solid geometry so long ago? *Sub specie aeternitatis.* The idea was that if you looked at the moment in a long perspective, in view of the final judgment, it was harder to do stupid things. "Hard, but not impossible," Big Al had added. (Little Albert taught English and put before them the style of *Time* magazine as the ultimate model of the language. *Time* was Republican in those days, so this called for some justification. Little Al's rejoinder was that how you said it had nothing to do with what you say. Three decades of police work had proved to Manfredi that that was bunk.) *Sub specie aeternitatis,* Big Al had advised. Five years later he married the nurse who had looked after him when he broke his foot. Still, it was good advice if you wanted to take the zest out of life. Ask yourself what anything will seem ten years hence? Had Lilian the poet lain in this room and pondered what for her had been the unpredictable future and was now the inscrutable past?

In one of the smaller bedrooms the ceiling fixture had a propeller design. The son's room. Somehow Manfredi detected no trace of the poet in the kitchen, The garage could be entered from the back hallway and there was a greenhouse attached. Its floor was several feet below the level of the garage's floor, and a little flight of steps ended in the bricked floor, the bricks not mortared, but artfully arranged in sand.

4

"Maybe you were right," Noonan said on Monday.

"How so?"

"The professor knows nothing. It's all gossip."

"She must have a theory of what happened."

"And you know what it is. Lilian and Ambrose Hennessy. She just knows there was something going on there."

"So the lady ran away from both her husband and her boyfriend."

"Rachel says there had to be a plan and something went

wrong. When we understand that we will understand everything."

"She's a lot of help."

"If you want to drop it, that's okay with me."

"You want to vote, Gloria?"

"That's why we marched and protested."

"Should we go on?"

Her lower lip rolled pinkly outward and she squeezed her
eyes shut. When she shook her head, her dangling earrings
swung like pendulums.

"Well, as Lincoln said to his cabinet, my vote trumps. I say
we continue."

"What for?"

"I've been reading Lilian Dahl's poems."

5

Brother Albert, Little Al, had pushed Byron and Keats,
but given Shelley a pass. A parody in the school paper, Ode
on a Grecian Urinal, had ignited Little Al. Only buffoons
made fun of things they didn't understand. Lilian had a poem
called "Forever He Pursues."

An eighteenth century nightingale
Makes lovers' music dear,
But crickets are of no avail
Racketing in the ear.
Our sessions ask for sun,
Some song from daytime birds
Each chirp a feathered sanction
More meaningful than words.

Gloria frowned. Noonan looked doubtful. Manfredi

agreed. "It's a lousy poem. Which is why she never published it. It could be called 'Little Emily.' "

"Where did you find it?"

"The girl who works for Bauer let me see some of the stuff he's been saving."

"Why did you pick this one?"

"Not only is it a bad poem, it employs a hackneyed device. Look at the opening letters of the lines."

Noonan did, saying them aloud. A microsecond went by before he saw it.

"Well, I'll be damned. Ambrose M."

Virginia

1

She supposed that other readers identified themselves with the authors they loved. There were Norman Mailers and John Updikes in creative writing classes she had taken. Women had a weakness for Sylvia Plath, drawn to tragedy. Virginia had known nothing of Lilian Dahl's mysterious disappearance when she first became hooked on her poetry. But from the beginning she had felt an eerie affinity with her. And she was eternally grateful to her mother who had given her a copy of the poems.

"But this is autographed."

"I want you to have it anyway."

Audrey had worked at the library in Benson while Virginia was growing up. That is where her father met her. "He came to take out a book and he took out me."

But Virginia had always thought it had been Audrey's decision. What on earth had she seen in Virginia's colorless father? He was a pharmacist, his visit to the library had been one of the few he had ever made; he lived in astonishment that he had won a wife like Audrey.

"But that's why," Audrey had said, when Virginia found some way to express her surprise that her parents had married. "I wanted a literal man, utterly without imagination and with a specialized intelligence."

"Why?"

"It is less complicated."

On her dresser Audrey kept photographs of her sister's children, a boy and a girl. They were all dead, the sister, her son and daughter, the brother-in-law too. Audrey loved to read but had no desire to collect books. She seemed to lack the acquisitive instinct entirely.

"Where did you get it?" Virginia asked, holding the book of Lilian Dahl's poems between her joined palms as if it were a prayer book.

"Someone donated it to the library. We already have a copy."

"But autographed?"

"They don't know the difference. I wanted you to have it. I used to like her things."

"Used to."

"I've grown out of poetry."

She grew out of life with Virginia's father too. After the divorce, by whose terms Virginia's father got custody of her, Audrey moved to California. Librarians can get jobs anywhere.

"That's what I'm going to be."

It was one of the few times she had seen her mother cry. It was the last time she saw her. A week after she arrived in California she was involved in an accident on the coastal highway. By the time they learned of it, it was too late to go out for the funeral, not that Virginia was sure they would have anyway. Whenever she read the poetry of Lilian Dahl, she felt in communication with her mother.

It was later, when her own marriage was going bad, that the realization came. She felt like a fool for not seeing it before. There had been the thought that it was Lilian's disappearance that sanctioned her mother's decision to leave her father. Now the autographed copy of the poems seemed a coded message, one her mother assumed she would one day decipher. Virginia never let the book out of her possession now. It was her talisman. Looking at the signature, comparing it with her mother's handwriting, she convinced herself that Audrey had deliberately disguised her hand. There must be scientific tests of such matters, but Virginia would not have subjected the matter to such an arbiter. Her growing faith that she was the daughter of Lilian Dahl had all the evidence it needed already.

2

"Have you ever thought of writing yourself?"

"I suppose everyone in English has."

Professor Hennessy smiled. "That, thank God, is not the case, my dear."

My dear. Virginia was used to the way men responded to her, particularly cultivated men, older men. Ambrose Hennessy was not just another man, of course. He had known Lilian and been very close to both her and to Basil. And here he was in old age, retired, living in the same retirement home as Basil. Is this where Lilian had been meant to live as well? No wonder she had gone.

Virginia found it an absorbing task to figure out what had been the relations among these people. Rachel Salma had figured in it, too, and not just on the edge. She seemed to be in love with both Basil and Ambrose. Absent from the published poems, except for one possible sly reference ("her rubeat aureole, seen in sun/invites an unkind question . . ."), there were many references in the papers, once certain correlations were seen. A longish unfinished poem called "The Dyer's Hand" was a satirical portrait of a nosy woman "whose carrot hair is hard upon the eyes." The poem put Rachel Salma before the reader's eye, even an eye that had seen her only in old age. With that, the many references to Dyer in the papers delivered up their meaning.

There was no similar indirection in the case of Ambrose Hennessy. He was simply a man and he clearly fascinated Lilian.

"What have you written?" Ambrose asked.

"I said I had thought of writing, not that I have. Does a dissertation count as writing?"

"More often it counts against it. You're writing on Lilian Dahl."

"Yes."

"You've come to the right place."

"You knew her, didn't you?"

"Insofar as one can know a poet."

"Now that is an interesting remark."

"You are very lucky Basil has given you access to the papers."

"That just happened. I agreed to help him computerize his papers, and I found myself confronted with things of Lilian Dahl's. Of course, I had told Basil of my interest in her."

"And, of course, Basil knew you would come upon Lilian's papers."

She ducked her head and looked up at him. "I hope you don't think that's what I had in mind."

"Heaven forbid. Did Basil tell you about the importunate Felicia Christman? Or the insistent Ben Ventuti?"

"Who are they?"

"How each in his different way would be wounded by your question. They are, or were, writers of reputation, both of them. And they had set their mind on writing the life of Lilian. Ventuti specializes in fast lives of ephemeral entertainers. One of his subjects had quoted Lilian in her suicide note. He looked into her life and came knocking on Basil's door."

"Do you mean the Felicia Christman who wrote on Willa Cather and Edna St. Vincent Millay?"

"The same."

"She won a prize."

Professor Hennessy smiled. "I will bet you did well in your comprehensive exams. Yes, she won both a Pulitzer and a National Book Award."

"And Basil turned her down."

"Emphatically. She criticized Cather for her apparent rectitude and celebrated the hedonism of Millay. He was not likely to deliver the memory of Lilian into such hands."

"I wondered why there has been no biography."

"They didn't need Basil's approval to write of Lilian, of course, but their only access to her was us, and any papers Basil might have."

"I never heard of Ventuti. Has Felicia Christman published anything lately?"

"They both regard the impasse they encountered when they wanted to write about Lilian as the rock on which their careers foundered. Ventuti would not take no for an answer, hung around the Fort Elbow campus for several years and mistook the liberated attitude of coeds as an invitation. He acquired quite a reputation. When one girl accused him of attempted rape, an Aristophanic chorus joined in. Given the kind of books he wrote, a prison sentence might seem a credit, but it ended his career. He blames it all on Basil."

"And Felicia?"

"She had assured both her editor and her agent that her next book would be on Lilian Dahl. A contract had been offered on that basis, a sizeable advance paid, and then—nothing. If Ventuti was persistent, Felicia considered it her destiny to write of Lilian. She refused to believe that Basil could stand fast against the stars. He did. She had a breakdown."

"How sad."

"I've always been surprised that one or both of them didn't seek revenge on Basil."

"Harm him?"

"Kill him."

3

"Sometimes," Basil said, "I have the feeling when we're talking that Lilian has come back to me."

"That's the nicest thing you could possibly say."

Virginia had found him so easy to get along with from the very beginning. He would tell her later that the day she came to interview for the job of research assistant he had the eerie feeling that his wife had returned.

"Do I look like her?"

"Only to someone who knew Lilian well."

How often Virginia had pored over photographs of her mother and the book jacket portrait of Lilian, willing them to be the same person. Thank God she had not had access to Basil's photograph albums earlier. There was no way the woman in all those snapshots could have been Virginia's mother. The fantasy was easier to relinquish when she had become close to Basil.

Old men have a susceptibility to young women. This was verified in Ambrose's half-fatherly, half-flirty attitude toward her.

"I'd been about to ask you myself," he said when Basil told him in Virginia's presence that he intended to marry Virginia. Ambrose had arrived wearing the look of a man with a mission. Of course he would consider it a duty to talk sense to Basil.

"I would have given you the same answer."

Basil chuckled. "I am glad I did not give up."

She would have been content for things to go on as they were. Getting married was his idea. The move to an office had been important, to get the papers and letters and albums and all the rest of it where she could work on them without tiring Basil. He was a dear to be with, but of course he wanted to talk and reminisce rather than let her work. She could not be impatient with him. After all, some of what he had to say was relevant to her work. It was the sense that she was taking advantage of him that bothered her. His infatuation with her, as a woman, mitigated that somewhat, and then she found herself feeling differently toward him.

Of course it was complicated. It was impossible not to see him as an icon, the husband of Lilian Dahl. It was equally impossible to overlook the fact that he was seventy-two years old. It had been a necessity that the office have a bathroom, given the frequency with which he relieved himself.

"In the immortal words of Cardinal Richelieu," he would say by way of preface to his going. The cardinal was alleged to have said that a gentleman ought never to pass a pissoir without using it.

"Is that why it's called a loo?"

He had a lovely melodious laugh. It was one of things Lilian had loved about him. The rondel, "The Key of B," immortalized Basil's laughter.

"What is it like to have a poem written about you?"

"It is something like a public hanging. If it weren't for the honor you would be willing to forego all the attention."

With intimacy came further confidences. Basil was content to hold her in his arms, to lay his face on her breast, to kiss her forehead and cheeks and nose. The question of what marriage could mean, of course, arose.

"Let me worry about that, Basil."

"So you don't think I am capable."

"I am sure you are." She moved her hand and under its caress he began to stir. "See?"

"Don't stop now."

She had stopped but that gesture restored Basil's male confidence.

"Lilian and I lived as brother and sister for more than a year."

"When?"

"Just before she left."

Virginia waited, conscious that he was about to tell her something known hitherto only to God and Lilian. He spoke so softly she lay her head on his chest and was reminded of what he had said of Ambrose and a stethoscope.

"It is a sign of love to want to forego rather than possess. That was my motivation. I didn't want her to bear more children. Giving birth came very hard for her. Making love to her was marvelous, Virginia. She was the only woman I had ever loved so I wasn't comparing her to this one or that one. I just knew that no one else could be like her. She was quite passionate. When what she called the 'yielding mood' was on her."

"That's Joyce."

"I didn't know that."

"From *The Dead*."

"I keep forgetting you're writing a dissertation."

"I would be willing to forego it."

He grasped her to him as if he were a young man, and when they kissed he cupped her breast. It was the closest they had come to anticipating the joys of marriage. His phrase.

"You will not forego anything. And neither, apparently, will I."

He moved her hand to the hard evidence of his virility.

4

A casualty of things going so well with her research on Lilian Dahl, and then the way things developed with Basil, was her friendship with Chip.

"Chip?" she had asked when she met him.

"My surname is Bufalo."

She waited but that seemed to be it.

"I guess you have to be a westerner to get it."

"Are you?"

"Pocatello."

She stepped back to take a better look. They were in the laundry room of the building where she had rented an apartment when she arrived in Fort Elbow to begin graduate studies in English on the campus associated with Lilian Dahl. That had been in August. This was November. The first thing to be said about Chip was that he wouldn't be mistaken for any of the guys in her classes. He wore a suit, he wore a shirt, he had a necktie on. Not dressed up, his working clothes. He was a writer at a local television station.

"What do you write?"

"Whatever is read on air. News, mainly."

"How did you get into that?"

"I wanted to read the stuff, not write it. I'm not pretty enough to be on camera."

He wasn't pretty at all. And he was big—tall, broad-chested and with a head that seemed even larger because of the wild profusion of hair. His face seemed to have been roughed out in clay and then left that way.

"And now you're doing laundry?"

"Somebody has to."

"Your turn?"

"Every time."

That answered her question, she guessed. Suddenly Virginia was aware how lonely these past months had been. She was doing what she wanted to do, and that was fine, but she didn't particularly like the academic company she kept and had made no friends. She didn't want to be friends with most of the other graduate students. The women were edgy and profane, ready to take offense, and the males were given to facetious arguments about texts that made you wonder why you would ever want to read anything. The authors Virginia liked knew what they had meant to say, said it, and your job was to grasp it. The new theory was that the author and his supposed intention were dispensable. A text is what you make it.

When she told Chip what she was doing he said his favorite author was Louis L'Amour. She could have cheered. They went upstairs and she made popcorn and over that and beer they talked about the Sacketts. He was divorced, that's why he had left Pocatello. He had been in front of the camera there, but the divorce had not been a calculated career move, and he took what work there was in the field he found familiar.

They became friends. They went out to eat a few times. When he came home late, he would tap on her door and she would put popcorn in the microwave. She was reading Trollope and told him that Ann Prettyman had said she hoped Major Grantley had popped to Grace Cawley. What did she mean? "Proposed." Chip's reaction surprised her.

"Popcorn. Popped. That's all I meant."

He seemed relieved. Obviously he had taken what she said as a heavy-handed hint. She couldn't have that.

"Chip, when I want to say something, I'll say it, all right?"

"I enjoy being with you."

"Let's keep it that way."

But it is not in the nature of things for a man and woman to become friends the way two men or two women might. She trimmed his mustache, she vetoed a tie he was about to buy, she helped him pick out a new frame when he had his eyes tested. He took to kissing her cheek on meeting and parting. And one night they started necking on the couch and eventually she led him into her bedroom. She lied when she told Basil later that Virginia was her condition as well as her name. While she was at it she lied about having had her imaginary child by artificial insemination.

The allusion to Trollope had been a warning. With Chip she forgot all about what occupied her mind. When they talked books it was westerns and that was fine with her. Out of superstition she did not mention that she was going to apply for the position Basil Bauer had advertised through the departmental secretary. The kind of chortling that went on around the bulletin board when others read about the job made her hope the competition would not be fierce. She wanted the job so much it frightened her. But she got it. Then she told Chip.

"What kind of a job is that? I thought you were preparing to teach."

"Chip, I've years to go before I finish. This is a part-time job. And it involves papers of the poet I'm writing on."

His face always looked sad, but it seemed sadder now. "I was getting ready to pop."

This time it was Virginia who did not catch the allusion.

"Uh-uh," she said when she did. "Things are fine the way they are."

"Maybe not."

He was like talking to a Sackett. She felt a strong urge to placate him, to minimize the importance of the opportunity Basil Bauer had given her, but that was out of the question. She had not rethought her life and come to Fort Elbow to sign on to whatever cruise Chip Bufalo was on. He didn't know himself.

"I'm sorry you feel that way."

And so began the decompression process, out of intimacy into just friends or strangers, the choice was his. He chose strangers. And blamed her for leading him on. In his angry version, she had made the first move, she had pursued him, she had led him to her bed. And then he hit her. Hard. Bringing his hand in a wide arc right into her face. It tipped her off her chair and when she scrambled to her feet, she tried to escape, but he had grabbed hold of her hair and held her back painfully. Virginia was terrified. The huge gentle man was now a threatening giant. And then he pushed her into the bedroom.

Hours later, she lay listening to him leave the apartment, and then she hurried naked to the door and locked it. Back in bed she stared at the ceiling, thinking how easily the same act can change from love to hatred, from tender union to violent possession.

5

Three days later she killed him.

She waited because she wanted to act with a cool mind. This was an execution, not an irrational act. On Wednesday he worked late. She was waiting for him in his apartment, not that he knew that. She had flicked the switches in the fuse box so that when he came in, no lights went on. He was drawn to the window she had opened and through which cold winter air entered his apartment. When he went to close the window she came up behind him with a baseball bat. She struck him three times on the head before he slumped to the floor. Then came the hard part, hoisting him onto the sill of the open window, his head and arms hanging out. She got behind him then, and as she was about to grab his legs he kicked out, his shoe driving into her stomach. She pushed against his foot, anger and pain and fear multiplying her strength. It was a struggle but she had the advantage. Neither of them spoke through the final battle that ended when he dropped silently five stories to the concrete areaway below.

Manfredi

Noonan brought in a photocopy of the newspaper story and laid it on Manfredi's desk. "Recognize her?"

The story was of a suicide months ago. Noonan was pointing to a girl in the background of the picture, residents of the building where the suicide had occurred.

"It could be anyone."

"It's the woman the professor hired."

"It doesn't even look like her."

"It's not a great picture, but I interviewed her at the time. I worked on that case."

"You interviewed everyone in the apartment building. You interviewed everyone at the television station where the guy worked. You just happen to remember her."

"She is beautiful. You can't tell by this picture. Of course I remember her. Would I forget Gloria?"

The secretary gave her slow smile, the one that revealed her teeth one at a time until the whole keyboard was on display. "Now you stop that."

"So what made you look up this story?"

He had done a Lexus search, feeding in all the names involved in the disappearance of Lilian Dahl. He had added Virginia Hardie's name to the search, and this was her first appearance in print.

"First."

"The other day there was a story about her research."

69

"Did I see that, Gloria?"

"What are we talking about?"

"A story about Virginia Hardie."

"Don't know nothing about it."

Noonan had clipped this story from the Sunday magazine in the local paper. No wonder Manfredi hadn't seen it. He never read the Sunday paper; he avoided all the Sunday morning political programs. Weekends were for sports, and he didn't want them disturbed by the sort of thing that made weekdays awful.

It was a nice spread, with a huge, soulful photograph of Basil Bauer. If you hadn't known Rachel Salma in the flesh, you might think she was a handsome woman from the picture of her. Ambrose Hennessy scowled into the camera. There was a cameo photograph of Lilian Dahl and another of Virginia Hardie, the girl Noonan had apparently fallen in love with.

"What did she have to do with the suicide?"

"Nothing. She just lived in the same building. And she knew the guy."

In the story of the suicide of Chip Bufalo, Virginia Hardie seemed to be the only resident that admitted knowing him. He had talked to her of his unsuccessful efforts to get back in front of the camera. Writing text for the idiot board was not what he wanted to do the rest of his life. The body had been shipped to Pocatello, Idaho, where the deceased had family and a burial plot.

In the story that had appeared in the Sunday magazine, the focus was on the papers that Virginia Hardie was helping Professor Bauer computerize. Among those papers were many belonging to the professor's late wife, the legendary poet Lilian Dahl, who had mysteriously disappeared thirty years ago. Bauer praised the work Virginia was doing, adding that he himself found it painful, even after all these years, to stir up sad memories.

"Nice picture of Professor Salma."

"Yeah."

"Let's have her in for a talk."

Rachel

1

Oh, the theories they had come up with at first, before Basil showed them Lilian's note. Amnesia, of course. Lilian still alive but not knowing who she was. Did that sort of thing really happen? Rachel was skeptical, and it would not do to mention Alzheimer's, as Ambrose did. But then such speculation had to be a game with Ambrose. Rachel was certain he knew. The note? On reflection she decided that anyone could write a note. It is difficult to be a single woman among eligible men and be constantly outshone by a married woman. Lilian had always assumed that men would be attracted to her. Hers was a disinterested certainty; all she needed was admission of her supremacy. Then the victim could be passed on to another woman.

"Have you ever read Kierkegaard's *The Diary of a Seducer*?" Rachel had once asked Lilian.

"A dirty book?"

"Far from it. It is a profound study of the sensuous. In its more advanced, that is to say corrupt form, seduction does not involve the body."

"I don't understand a word of that."

Rachel came to believe these protestations of ignorance on Lilian's part. Not ignorance, lack of learning. There was so much she had not read and had no intention of reading, even in poetry. The influences on her were few but decisive.

"The Bible, of course. And the hymnal. And John Bannister Tabb."

"John Bannister Tabb!"

"Do you know him?"

Rachel wondered if this were a quid pro quo for her mentioning Kierkegaard. She even suspected that Lilian was inventing the poet, but there was such a man. Ambrose knew all about him.

"He was a priest, Rachel. A southerner for whom the Civil War was a central event."

Lilian did have Babette Deutsch's book on prosody and the anthology of Tate and Warren. This explained the variety of forms she used—the canzone, the rondel. And there were several clerihews, more influence of Ambrose Hennessy. If Lilian had a literary mentor it was Ambrose. Ambrose and Basil had been friends from their early teens; Lilian had called them systole and diastole. Ambrose discovered her when she enrolled as a special student. He was drawn to the lovely girl seated alone in a corner in the student center and pulled out a chair and sat down when she, to his question "What are you doing?" answered, "Writing a poem." On the table before her was only a cup half full of now-cooled coffee. She sat with folded arms, a serene expression and had not been, as Ambrose had thought, looking at him intently. She had been repeating to herself a poem she had written the day before, trying to discover what it needed.

"Recite it for me."

The poem was the lovely, "A Narrow Time," suggested by one of the many that Emily Dickinson had written at the bedside of dying friends.

Out of the shallows of my soul
I cry, O Lord, to thee,
Grateful that the shadows fall
On someone else, not me.

73

Why am I surprised to learn
When fasting can be food
That that same alchemy can turn
My grief to gratitude.

Ambrose had recounted the conversation to Rachel as if nothing could intrigue her more than a girl who had intrigued him. Basil had found his enthusiasm more contagious, and Basil had the advantage of being in history rather than literature. Lilian was not interested in the kind of course Ambrose taught, but Basil on the Enlightenment captivated her. She was even more captivated by the mini-course he offered between semesters on Captive Popes. Who but Basil would have known or cared about the many popes who had been kidnapped or imprisoned throughout the centuries? Basil put her onto Paul Claudel, which led to the very long and, Ambrose said, though it was not a criticism, imitative ode. Basil's Catholicism was grounded in history, Ambrose's in literature and art. Lilian stated her intention of becoming a Catholic when she married Basil, two months after they met. And eventually she did become "a Catholic of a sort," as she put it.

If there could be the equivalent of a salon in Fort Elbow, Ohio, Lilian began one after her marriage. And her poems began to appear, as if they, rather than the son and daughter who eventually came, were the fruit of the marriage.

2

"I sound like the chronicler of her life, don't I?" Rachel said to Detective Noonan. The police were finally showing some interest in reopening the inquiry into Lilian's disappearance.

"Why is it you who insists on reopening the inquiry?"

"I want to be exonerated."

"Exonerated?"

"Well, think of it. Whether or not I like it, Lilian is going to be read into the indefinite future. There will be curiosity about her life, her friends and, above all, about her disappearance. The three of us were rightly the ones questioned as to what might have happened. Basil, of course. A husband ought to have some notion of where his wife might go if she went away."

"How did she leave, by the way? I assume she didn't drive, since there is no record that a vehicle was traced."

"Who knows? But public transportation was still readily available then, trains and buses departing in all directions many times each day."

"And tickets were anonymous?"

"Completely. Nowadays, if you fly to Minneapolis it is entered into a computer and becomes, I suppose, a permanent record. Computers have destroyed privacy."

"They would have made it an easier matter to trace where she went."

"If she went."

"You doubt it?"

"Anyone can doubt it. Anyone can imagine anything. They can imagine that Basil or Ambrose or I, singly or in various combinations, did away with her."

"Killed her?"

"Killed her. I have long thought that Ambrose Hennessy knows a good deal more than he has ever said."

"More than the husband?"

"More than the husband."

"Captain Manfredi noticed that one of her love poems is dedicated to Ambrose Hennessy. Is his middle initial M?"

"M for Martin. What poem are you talking of?"

He had it with him, a photocopy, with the initials of each line ringed. He seemed fearful she would ask him to read it. They were seated in the recreation room at the Residenza, at a table where bridge was played, and her knee was inadvertently pressed against his. He had the very black hair of the Irish, blue eyes with lashes like a girl's, but the jutting jaw bristled with whiskers.

"I wonder if anyone else ever noticed that."

"You didn't?"

"No. I suppose Ambrose knew but he was hardly likely to call attention to it. Your captain discovered this?"

"Manfredi."

"I've met him."

"He wants to meet you again. I am to ask if you would mind coming to his office to talk about all this."

"Am I a suspect?"

"If you wish."

He had a lovely, wicked smile, but when he helped her rise it was painfully obvious that he was deferring to age, not gender.

3

Michigan City, Indiana. A town that sounded as if it did not know what state it was in, ambiguous enough to be attractive to Jews. There was a large and cohesive Jewish community in Michigan City, ranging from professionals, entrepreneurs, shopkeepers, to junk dealers. Rachel's father fought a losing battle against the chains and malls. His neighborhood grocery, with the store downstairs, living quarters upstairs, was a prize when he took possession, paying top dollar, but going downhill ever since.

"Abe, you shoulda asked."

"I shoulda asked. You were where at the time, Rose, in Peru?"

"Any idiot shoulda known the destiny of this part of town."

"Don't give me that destiny."

Her brother Herbert was the apple of their eye, a whiz at school, he rattled off Hebrew at his Bar Mitzvah like a rabbi. Her parents were not that wild when Herbert said he wanted to be a rabbi. It was fine that he believed all that, but let's not lose our heads. The community offered an Abraham Herschel scholarship and with his brains Herbert was a cinch to get it. Be a doctor, make a little money, look after the old folks, is that asking a lot? Herbert answered in Hebrew, and they knew it was more destiny. No one much noticed Rachel.

She walked away with the Abraham Herschel, straight A's all those years, and she wrote an essay on the diaspora that was nearly taken by *Commentary*. When the editors decided against it, maybe thinking of all the bright kids out there writing publishable papers, the Jewish community brought it out as a pamphlet. Abe and Rose couldn't figure it out. Rachel a big brain? Well, big by Michigan City standards. She was accepted by Bradley University in Peoria, Illinois, and before they put her on the train, Rose came into her room, shut the door and told her she was a darling girl but she should know she wasn't theirs; she might not even be Jewish, it was impossible to tell. A boy, she'd be circumcised, but a girl? Anyway, they loved her and would miss her in the store, but study hard and trust in God.

If Michigan City was confused, how about her? Whether she was Jewish or Gentile she didn't know. Rose seemed to think it gave her a better chance, the chance that she wasn't Jewish, but with a name like Rachel Solomon no one was going to think she came from Ireland. She changed it to Salma to confuse the issue more.

Where had she come from? Tenants in an apartment house Abe owned complained about a baby crying, phoning him in the middle of the night, and he went over because the apartment they were complaining about was empty, but the baby was there, wrapped up, on the floor, wailing away. Abe picked it up and it stopped crying so he took it back to the store and had a helluva fight with Rose who thought what Rachel did when Rose told her the story. Abe had something going on the side and she was the result? Rose knew him too well really to believe that, but she gave him hell anyway, bringing home a crying baby in the middle of the night, what were they supposed to do with it?

Listening to this, knowing Abe and Rose, having tuned into their ongoing nonstop argument all her life, Rachel knew it could have gone either way, keep the kid or turn her in wherever you did. The contingencies of life. The vagaries of fate. At the University of Minnesota she wrote her doctoral dissertation on Browning's "Rabbi Ben Ezra" and landed a job at the Fort Elbow campus.

4

"And met Hennessy and Bauer?"

Captain Manfredi had settled back in his chair after Noonan presented her. Such deference they showed her. But were they serious? The captain had discovered Ambrose's name hidden in a love poem and his curiosity was piqued. There was a crossword on the desk, so he liked puzzles, but what was his attention span?

"Oh, I knew them both before. We are all alumni of the University of Minnesota."

"They hired three of you at once?"

"Hennessy came first and then Basil was hired. Ambrose called to tell me of the opening. He had done that for Basil as well."

"Noonan tells me you want to exonerate yourself."

"Captain, I would like to know what really happened. This mystery has been hanging over our lives for thirty years. We talk about it but we don't really talk about it. Basil must blame Ambrose; I know I do. Maybe they both blame me."

"Why would they blame you?"

"Because I saved her life once."

Manfredi tucked in his chin in surprise. "How did you do that?"

Lilian had come to Professor Hennessy's office unannounced, just walked in although he was talking to a student, and began to speak in a drawling voice. Ambrose thought she was drunk so he shagged the other student out and put Lilian in the chair. She kept talking goofy and looked drowsy. Ambrose, of course, was thinking what the student he had sent away would make of all this, so he told Lilian to just sit there and came next door to Rachel's office. She wasn't there. The departmental secretary didn't know where she had gone; she had been there ten minutes before. Five minutes passed, ten minutes, Ambrose was worried that Lilian would come reeling out of his office, and he would have the secretary as well as that student spreading stories about him. He was about to ask the secretary to come back with him when Rachel returned. ,

"I went to his office with him. Lilian was on the floor. I looked at Ambrose and he looked at me. Her skirt was well above her knees and she looked, well, vulnerable. As soon as I knelt beside her I knew what it was."

"What?"

"A diabetic coma. I dug around in her purse and found the insulin and syringe and gave her an injection."

"Are you diabetic?"

"Yes. That's a secret. The injection helped, but we got her over to the student infirmary where they kept her overnight. It had been serious. I was given credit for saving her life."

"And you think she held that against you?"

"There are diabetics who spend most of their lives kidding themselves that they aren't. They feel so wonderful they skip their shots, maybe the whole thing has passed, and the next thing you know they are reeling around like Lilian."

"You're not that kind?"

"I am the kind who admits it to herself but to nobody else."

"Ambrose and Basil don't know you're a diabetic?"

"Certainly not."

Noonan wanted to know why saving Lilian's life would bring Rachel under suspicion.

"Because I knew how easily she could be killed. Withhold insulin, she would be dead."

"But you didn't do that?"

"Would I be insisting that you reopen the investigation if I thought the result would be my indictment?"

"To answer a question with a question is not to answer the question."

Ambrose

1

Seasons become less distinct as one grows old. Memories of mild winters and chill summers blur the line between elemental hot and cold. Only autumn retains its metaphoric force, providing the objective meteorological correlative of oneself withering and becoming sere.

"Strange word," Virginia murmured.

"Not if you know Latin."

"I envy that in you and Basil."

"Has he told you of Dowling Hall?"

"Was that the name of the school?"

"It no longer exists."

The religious order, a species of the Franciscans, that had founded and operated the prep school that Hennessy and Bauer attended, had withstood the world, the devil and the flesh, but they were undone by the aggiornamento decreed by Vatican II. The perpetual vows they had taken were renegotiated and they left the order, one by one at first, then in groups. Hennessy still found the story all but incredible, but he and Basil had heard it from the lips of Old Piety himself, Father Pius, a throb in his voice as he reported like the servant in Job. "I alone have escaped to tell you." Teachers of the sort required to keep the curriculum that had made the school famous were hard to come by. Tuition rose as quality fell. The exodus that had begun with the faculty spread to the student body. Franciscans had not concerned themselves with an endowment; what would *il Poverello* have said to laying up treasure on earth? Debts were incurred, credit stretched to the breaking point, the will to survive seeped away. Shrewd bankers got the property for a pittance. Pius was passing through on pilgrimage to Assisi. When they put him on the plane it was like saying goodbye to the past.

"I didn't realize that schools can die." There was wonder in Virginia's voice.

"Where is Basil?"

"Taking a nap. I have a question."

I have a question. Ambrose looked at Virginia. Was she deliberately employing the words Lilian had used when she came to him before marrying Basil? Who knew what the girl was finding among those papers Basil had hoarded over the years? Lilian could have kept a diary, for all Ambrose knew. She had kept a notebook, spiral bound with lined pages, there must be dozens of those. Had she noted down things that happened, conversations? Only a heedless poet would have made a record of the conversation that had begun with "I have a question."

"You want to know what I think of your marrying Basil?" Ambrose had answered Lilian.

"Am I that transparent?"

Lilian had suggested that by marrying Basil she was getting two for the price of one; she would be even more closely tied to Ambrose.

"Then marry me, not him."

"He is serious, are you?"

If it was a dare, he did not take it. There are remembered moments to which one goes back again and again, perhaps forever, wanting to occupy once more the point where things went one way but might have gone another. Would boldness have won her or repelled her? Would she have thought him a faithless friend if he had tried to win her then, after she had accepted Basil?

"Why are you testing me?"

"Is that what I'm doing?"

"I don't know what you're doing."

She sat with her hands in her lap looking at him. "You saw me, you saw what happens to me, what can happen any time I forget to measure out my life in insulin. Basil never saw that."

"Rachel did."

"Rachel." She shrugged her savior away as an irrelevancy. "I think that gives you a claim over me."

"It is Rachel you should be grateful to."

"I am not talking of gratitude."

He had decided before this that conversations with her were not to be understood along usual lines. She was a poet; this could never be forgotten. She was possessed of a special membrane that responded incommensurately to things and people around her. The world was what she experienced, felt, imagined; she was not interested in any independent existence it might have. She did not deny it, she simply was not interested. To communicate with her required discerning what she imagined, not what was ostensibly being spoken of. She had been working mentally on a poem the first time he met her. But that was what she was always doing. The question she had come to pose before her marriage to Basil was like a preliminary sketch of a poem, a rough draft. What if . . .

They had their honeymoon, Ambrose and Lilian, a week before she married Basil. A fortnight later, Ambrose tried unsuccessfully to make love to Rachel.

"Your heart's not in it."

"That's not my heart."

"Well, that's my it. Get off."

83

He should have been embarrassed to talk of it. With anyone other than Rachel he would have been. But they were just two also-rans and he, at least, had run out of gas.

"Rachel, what would you say if I told you I loved Lilian?"

"You wouldn't want to hear."

"It's true."

"What have you been drinking?"

"Mineral water."

"It's turned you into an animal. You'd make a better vegetable."

"You're good enough a vegetable for me."

"Oh, ha ha."

Thus humor doth make heroes of us all.

2

"What are you afraid of, Virginia?"

"Lilian."

"She's dead."

"But does Basil think so?"

"Believe me, she's dead. It has nothing to do with what he thinks."

"What he thinks has a lot to do with my marrying him."

"Is that all?"

"What more do I need?"

"You've been married before, right?"

"Wrong, not right."

"Are you worried about going to bed with Basil?"

The expression she adopted was meant to be cute, and it was. "That does not worry me."

"It could be like marrying a monk."

"Because he's old?"

"There is old and old."

Another version of the cute expression. "What makes you such an authority?"

"I'm the other kind of old."

"But you never married."

"I was waiting to become old."

"You loved Lilian, didn't you?"

"Everybody loved Lilian."

"Come on."

"We had a conversation very much like this just before she married Basil."

"How did it end?"

"Don't rush me."

"Because you're old?"

"Because I am wise."

"Did you ever make love to Lilian?"

"If someone asked me that about you, would you want me to answer?"

"But she's dead."

"I'm not."

Would she or wouldn't she? With Lilian, years ago, in a similar situation, it had been passion and envy and resentment. And mutual. But he was wiser now, at least in the sense of older, and he wanted to know what she felt for Basil. He had no illusions about what Virginia felt for him.

"I respect you for not telling."

"You have discovered the motive for my silence."

"I mean it."

Being seduced is far more tiresome than seducing. Ambrose advanced, retreated, equivalently showed a little leg, covered his cleavage, feared aloud that she would no longer respect him. It was a relief when she settled into his lap, facing him, and they made independent love to whatever lay over the other's shoulder. Poor Basil.

3

Should he wait until after the wedding before talking to the police? The detective Noonan had spoken to Rachel and had asked for an appointment with Ambrose. An appointment. My dear fellow, let me check my calendar to see when I can fit you in. What did he think retirement means? Chekov said he didn't know what loneliness meant until he married. Ambrose had learned the meaning of the phrase, time on his hands. On his wrist too. Putting a new battery into his watch always raised the question of whether it would survive him or vice versa. The odds had been favoring the battery for quite some time.

Decisions should be made rationally. An exercise in practical reason. The principles or general guides of conduct; the singular facts of the here and now. From these the action should flow straightaway, all things being equal. That is, if one is rational. Hennessy opened a volume of Milton and with closed eyes pointed to the page. He opened them to read " . . . to sport with Amarylis in the shade." Let the nuptials begin.

Manfredi

1

It was a measure of his quickening interest in the matter that Manfredi accompanied Noonan to the retirement home where Basil Bauer, the husband of the woman who had walked away thirty years ago, was to marry a woman nearly a quarter of a century his junior.

"What's the point of getting married at his age?"

"What's the point of staying single?"

"Would he still be—capable?"

"Only his proctologist knows for sure."

When young people get married you don't look at them and think of them in bed doing it. You think of the years ahead, the trials and joys, kids, the whole ball of wax. But with someone Basil's age, sex, if there was any, would be a self-contained thing.

"Remember Abraham," Gloria said when he voiced a version of these thoughts in the office.

"How can I forget?"

"What did she mean by Abraham?" Noonan asked in the car.

"Maybe she meant Methuselah."

Noonan's frown deepened. Better let it go.

The old guy had spent a dollar or two on the wedding. The recreation room was full of flowers. The chairs in rows mimicked pews with a bouquet adorning the aisle seats. In front there was what reminded Manfredi of a May altar, lots of linen and candles and more flowers. It gave the place a churchy air. The judge was already there, wearing a gown which sported a festive corsage, her thick gray hair hanging to her shoulders, her bangs reaching to the tops of her glasses, showing lots of teeth as she smiled benevolently at the gathering audience. The men all favored their backs when they bent over, and there was a bow-legged fellow who seemed to have had a hip replacement and did not take a chair but kept on the move, maybe showing off. The women wore too much lipstick, usually the wrong shade, and dressed in what might be called party dresses, blues, pinks, several polka dots. No hats. Maybe because all the perms were new. Half of them, men and women, wore expressions of smiling expectancy, probably deaf as posts. In this bunch, Rachel didn't look all that bad.

Noonan went to say hello to Judge Wright. Manfredi stayed put. Judges were a necessary evil as far as he was concerned, appointed to make life difficult for the police. He had nothing against Wright in particular, but Noonan was wasting his time if he thought civil treatment would be repaid in kind when the chips were down and a trial was under way.

"I made a date to talk with her about the legal aspects of the Lilian Dahl disappearance," he told Manfredi when he returned. "The time lag and all."

"What do you think we have prosecutors for?"

"I've wondered."

"Some of the interns know a little law."

"They all know a little law," Noonan said, then grinned at what he had said.

That left the police. Manfredi had often thought that Justice wears a blindfold because she is about to pick a number from a bowl, pure chance.

"Can you operate this, darling?" Rachel, all gussied up

and thoroughly perfumed, was holding out a video camera to
Noonan.

"Sure."

He lifted the camera and it whirred briefly. Rachel threw
up her gloved hands in mock horror.

"Not of me. But everyone else."

"As if I were collecting evidence?"

"Oh you. I'm to be maid of honor."

"That is quite an honor."

"I didn't say honorary maid."

"Then say it."

The nametags didn't help much since only first names
were given in the space beneath HELLO!

"Don't they know one another?"

"Do you remember everyone you know?"

Ambrose Hennessy, who would be best man, and Basil appeared, wearing identical suits, but no one would mistake the
one for the other. Hennessy's hair was salt and pepper, worn
long, with undulations covering the tops of his ears. Bauer's
hair was cottony, his face pink, he looked like a boy, which
was in his favor since the bride was nearly a quarter century
younger. The two men, accompanied by murmurs and gig-
gles and whispers, went to the front and took up the positions
by the judge. A fat lady in a powder blue slack suit began
playing on an electric keyboard. And then the bride appeared
in the doorway, her arm through that of a priest in street
clothes. What the hell was this?

He was Father Herrick from the Newman Club on
campus, rumors of whose innovative liturgies had reached
Manfredi's disapproving ear. He learned later that Herrick
had offered to concelebrate with the judge and bless the
union sub rosa, but Basil had said no. Giving away the bride
put Herrick sufficiently in view; he was unwilling to pay too

high a price for playing by the rules. He brought Virginia up the aisle as if celibacy had just been abrogated and he was making an honest man of himself.

Manfredi drifted to the back to the tune of "Jesu, Joy of Man's Desiring." Noonan had the camera going and was sweeping the audience before turning the camera toward the front. The PA system emitted a few squeaks and complaints before Judge Wright mastered it and the ceremony began.

Judge Wright told them what they were about to do in case anybody had come to the wrong room. Here and there an ear was cupped, but that might have been mere habit. The wedding was over almost before it began. Take the Mass out of it, boil it down to the exchange of promises, and it is an affair of minutes, not an hour. The strains of Bach seemed still audible when the keyboard began to give them Lohengrin.

"I'm coming downtown to see you," Professor Hennessy said. "Early in the week."

"Good."

"About the first Mrs. Basil Bauer."

Manfredi groaned. He was sorry he had decided to reopen that. Here he was, wasting an afternoon at the wedding of people he didn't even know.

"I'll clear it all up."

"Sure."

"Monday. Tuesday."

"May be my good news day." His voice croaked, he couldn't carry a tune, but Hennessy got it and laughed.

2

"I killed her."

Hennessy wore a blue tweed sport jacket, black slacks and a blue shirt open at the collar. He looked twenty years younger than he was. He had come in, looked around the office, sat and made his confession.

"You killed her."

"Lilian Dahl. Basil's wife."

"You just remembered?"

"It's different now. He has a new wife, a new life. Lilian and I were lovers."

"I see."

"Before she married Basil. And the marriage didn't end it. But then she cut me off. If I had cut her off, something I wanted to do, planned to do, would have done, it would have been different, but the more she said no the more I wanted her."

"How long had she been married when she disappeared?"

"She disappeared because I killed her."

"Because she cut you off."

"Basil had decided they would live as sister and brother, so she wouldn't have any more children. If she wasn't sleeping with her husband, she wouldn't sleep with me either."

"Now that makes sense."

"She was a poet. Poets don't make sense. Try to reason with one, it can't be done. This went on for a year. It preyed on me. I thought of little else. I just could not accept Lilian's refusal."

"How did you kill her?"

"Damn it, I'm serious. Do you know what it has cost me to come here and finally confess?"

Manfredi suddenly saw how indulgent it had been to tell Noonan they would reopen the investigation into the missing Lilian Dahl. He should have known this would happen, people coming forward and claiming to know all about it, claiming they had killed her, at least in Hennessy's case. The professor might look younger than his years but he was a septuagenarian, distinguished, not credible in the role of killer. Imagine trying to convince the prosecutor they should build a case against Hennessy. Nobody got life anymore, and if he did he could figure it didn't mean much. The state prison or the retirement home, how much difference was there? Hennessy had no family. In prison, he could teach his fellow inmates, revive his career. But he wouldn't know that.

"Professor Hennessy, it doesn't cost you a thing to confess. I'll bet you've been rehearsing this. What is this, a wedding present to Bauer?"

Hennessy stared at him. "Of all the things I imagined about this scene, skepticism on your part was not one of them."

"How did you kill her?"

"I strangled her. It began as a kind of joke, to emphasize how frustrated I was, but once I began I didn't stop. She was so vulnerable. She thought I was joking too, until it was too late."

"What did you do with the body?"

"I buried it. Why are you smiling?"

"You're proving my point. Some people work on their alibis. You've obviously worked on your confession."

"I can show you where I buried her. I buried her in a greenhouse."

Manfredi could still see Hennessy as Bauer's best man the previous Saturday. Dapper, good looking, loving the spotlight. Had he imagined himself playing the role of confessed murderer? Maybe he thought the trial would get media coverage, even national coverage.

There was a knock, Manfredi said come in and Noonan did. He looked at Hennessy and then came and leaned close to Manfredi's ear.

"Rachel is here." Noonan whispered. "She says she killed Lilian Dahl."

After he stopped laughing, Manfredi stood and said to Hennessy. "Get the hell out of here. I have to listen to other people who claim to have killed Lilian Dahl."

"It's Rachel, isn't it?"

"You want to switch your story? You want to tell me you confessed to save Rachel?"

Hennessy's face was flushed and his voice trembled when he spoke. "I am going to your superior, Captain Manfredi. He ought to know how you react when a murderer turns himself in."

"Murderers, Hennessy. There's no reason to think anyone get murdered and I already have two murderers."

Virginia

1

During the first fortnight of her marriage to Basil—she just loved it when he spoke of fortnights and lustra and other odd measures of time—Virginia received so much mail. The main effect of the wedding seemed to have been to draw attention to the poet who had disappeared, Basil's first wife. His new wife, it was made clear, intended to help Basil keep the flame of remembrance burning. Some people sent money, many enclosed a clipping of the story that had appeared in the local paper. Two that did came from Felicia Christman and Ben Ventuti. Both were disposed to let bygones be bygones. Ventuti wrote of a new unspecified project, but said he would be glad to set it aside if she wanted a collaborator on the Lilian Dahl book. "I can give you details of my experience with editors and booksellers, and I have representation on both coasts, a New York agent for print, a California agent for film and television."

Felicia was at once more subtle and more threatening. "I had never hated another person until you usurped the role that Lilian Dahl had intended I should play. Now that you have usurped her role as Basil's wife you must give me back my reason for living. I wish you all happiness in your new marriage."

Virginia decided against showing these troubling messages to Basil. Marriage had brought on a state of euphoria. In bed, he wanted only to hold her, for now, and to fall asleep in her arms. Once in the night he had spoken in his sleep, addressing Lilian. Smiling, Virginia kissed his sleeping face, eased out of his embrace and drifted into sleep herself.

The first project, taking precedence over her dissertation and everything else, was to bring out a selection of the many unpublished poems Lilian had left. A credential infinitely more weighty than her dissertation would be a volume of Lilian's poems with Virginia's name, along with Basil's, as editor. Basil had suggested a preface, but Virginia objected. Nothing was more annoying than to pick up a classic and find that some critic had written an essay on it that was given pride of place in the new edition. What presumption.

"A postface, then. After the text, in the back of the book."

He wanted Virginia to write it. Diffidence washed over her at the thought and left her dizzy. She could bring no prestige to such a task. What she wanted to do was provide notes, give an indication of the discovery of the poem, its date, factual matter, in short. Despite her long immersion in it, Virginia was far from confident that she could write an interesting essay on Lilian's poetry.

After lunch she brought Basil to the office—mornings, she worked there alone—and wondered if she shouldn't show him the notes from Felicia Christman and Ben Ventuti. He read through both copies of the newspaper account of their wedding, but just glanced at the letters.

"Well?"

"Ventuti is obviously out of work, Virginia. This is a plea for permission to steal credit from you. Isn't that an old Hollywood trick—do anything to get one's name included in the credits of a film? He says nothing of what his collaboration would bring to the project. As with Felicia, this is a plea for you to go away and let her take over."

"I don't know how to answer them."

Basil removed the clippings from the envelopes, crushed the letters and dropped them into the wastebasket.

"That's how. So what is on the agenda today?"

"I wish all these papers could be published as they are."

"Maybe they will be, some day. The possibility is an added motivation. But for now a new book of poems will suffice."

"I'd like to publish all the poems anyway."

"Oh, my no. Some of them would tarnish her reputation. People might agree that even Homer nods, but mediocre work from a lesser author is unacceptable."

"I suppose Homer is more important."

"Compared to Homer, Lilian is a single, a double at most. She reached first on a bunt and stole second."

Lilian had loved baseball, a passion Virginia did not share. Nor apparently had Basil. It was Ambrose Hennessy who offered to take her to Cincinnati or Cleveland to see a game. If Basil had any intimation that something was going on between Lilian and Ambrose, he gave no hint of it. To Virginia, the evidence was clear. How odd that Ambrose should be best man at Basil's wedding.

"And for the second time."

"You were best man when Basil married Lilian?"

"Only in a manner of speaking."

It was because of what she knew about Lilian and Ambrose that Virginia had made love to him before she married Basil. The event retained its sharpness in memory because its only rival since the wedding was falling asleep in Basil's chaste embrace.

2

Would Basil have preserved this mound of material—notebooks, typescripts with several carbons, sometimes carbons without any corresponding ribbon copy, letters, mementos, books, what looked to be attempts at a novel—if he realized what a judgment it contained of him and of his marriage to Lilian? The deeper she got into the materials, the more Virginia wondered at Basil's fidelity to the memory of his wife. And the more incredible she found it that it came to be accepted that the powerful personality behind all this material had simply walked away.

"It used to seem too close," Basil said, after leafing through one of Lilian's notebooks. "Now it seems remote. Virginia, I am beginning to get over her."

He had pretty much left the papers to her before. Now, when he joined her at the office, he brought along what he was reading and settled down with that. He had decided to read again the volumes Winston Churchill had written on World War II and sat grumbling at his desk and making marginalia in the book while Virginia readied things for scanning into the computer.

"Why did he save it?" Alma fussed over the tea she had made. The invitation had come when Virginia telephoned to ask Alma a question. One did not gain access to Alma's view of the past that easily. "He is a historian."

"The way Churchill saved his government papers?"

"Lilian is not quite equal to World War II, but yes, something like that."

"You taught history, didn't you?"

"Yes. Ancient and medieval. Neither had been the focus of my graduate work. We had to be versatile in those days. You might be asked to teach almost anything and you had to be able to work up a class on it."

Alma wore white slacks and an extra large Ohio State sweatshirt that looked like a miniskirt on her. Dressed or casual, Alma had a girlish air.

"I am concentrating on the notebooks."

"Notebooks."

"There is a pile of them. All precisely dated on the covers. For example, Jan.–April, 1963. Some years involve as many as eight notebooks, others four."

"What's in them?"

"Once she called them her Commonplace Books. Notes on what she was reading, drafts of poems, diary entries."

"Does she refer to people?"

"Oh yes. You're in them."

"Good heavens. I'm afraid to ask more."

"Such entries usually just mention who she saw, what she did. A party, a chat with someone."

"How many notebooks in all?"

"Fifty-nine."

"Fifty-nine! I had no idea she was that industrious. She was what you would call cool. Laid back. Well, better not use that."

"Did you suspect her of infidelity?"

Alma smiled sweetly. "Let's say I never suspected her of fidelity."

"I can't believe Basil didn't know."

"Are the notebooks confessional?"

"In a matter of fact sort of way. But she uses code names for people, usually pretty obvious."

"Do I have a code name?"

"Yes. BB."

Alma held up her hand, to stop an explanation. "No. Let me guess. There was a Dick Tracy character—Dick Tracy was a silly comic strip that everybody read—called BB eyes. I hope that wasn't it."

"Betty Boop."

"Well!" But Alma smiled, on the whole pleased.

"She accuses you of flirting with Basil."

"Is that all?"

"Was there more?"

"Is that what you wanted to ask?"

"Oh, no."

"Keep me posted. Or I suppose you could just ask Basil."

"I wouldn't do that."

"To protect my reputation?"

What a hothouse culture a faculty had been in those days, and of course those days were the 1960s when things fell apart in the society as a whole and most particularly on college campuses. Virginia had read so much about the students of that time, the protests and marches and strikes, but a faculty is a more permanent feature on a campus than the students. There is a constant turnover of the student body, at that time in every sense of the phrase, but the principle of continuity is the faculty and Lilian's diary suggested a faculty running wild.

"I talked with Alma today, Basil."

"Such a lovely person."

"Cute as a button. Lilian calls her Betty Boop."

Basil laughed melodiously. "I had forgotten that. But then I had forgotten the original. I hope Lilian gave me credit. I was the first to call Alma that."

"In the notebooks, BB is quite a flirt."

"All women were flirts in those days, Virginia. And men aspired to be swingers. It's embarrassing to recall how silly we were."

"You must tell me of your conquests."

"That would be a story soon told." He closed his book on his finger, to mark the place. "Unless of course I chose Churchillian exaggeration. In retrospect I might say that I

99

was filled with foreboding during the time before Lilian disappeared."

"That did surprise you, didn't it, her going?"

"It still does."

3

Although Virginia had talked with Detective Noonan when Chip died—she had been interviewed along with everyone else in the building—he did not seem to remember their previous encounter. Or was he slyer than he seemed? During those dreadful days after Chip's body had been found, Virginia took her cue on how to react from the others in the building.

"You knew him, didn't you?" she had been asked.

"We all knew him."

"I had the impression that you two . . . Well, never mind."

Another tenant had noticed that she and Chip had been together a lot. There are so many snoopy people and this woman, puffy face, hair a mess, a pot belly that made her look pregnant although she had to be sixty, was just the kind that could be trouble.

"You knew him better than most," Detective Noonan had said when he talked with her.

"I can't tell you what a shock this has been."

"I suppose. Right out the window. I thought he might be on something. People drop a little acid and they think they can fly."

"Did he take drugs?"

"Nothing showed up. And there was no note."

"Could it have been an accident?"

"Maybe. He clawed up the sill before he dropped. Maybe he meant to take a dive and changed his mind."

Virginia hid her face in her hands. Noonan said he was sorry. Did she know anything that could be helpful in the investigation? She just shook her head and he left her and that was that. The verdict was suicide. It had a depressing effect on the building, and she wasn't the only one who decided to move even when they offered to hold her rent at the same level for another year. She did promise the manager to keep quiet about the suicide, a silly request, as it had been all over TV and in the paper. The news reader on Chip's station observed a moment's silence for his "fallen colleague," the unfortunate phrase the result of a try for the dramatic. Obviously he needed a Chip to put words in his mouth.

In her own mind, Virginia decided that Chip had committed suicide. She edited her memories of the scene in his kitchen until her own role completely disappeared.

Just when it all seemed behind her, she got a call from Detective Noonan.

"You moved."

"Yes."

"A funny thing. One of the keys Chip Bufalo had in his pocket was to your apartment."

"Oh, I gave him that."

A silence on the wire. Virginia laughed and was surprised how genuine it sounded.

"Don't be having bad thoughts. I gave it to him so that he could look in while I was away."

"You have a cat?"

He would know that she hadn't had a cat. "To water my plants."

"Ah. Well, you won't need this key."

"No."

"I'll give it to the manager."

"Good."

After she hung up she was so upset she actually trembled. She did not want to think of Chip anymore, of what had happened to him, and why it had happened. She did not want the police thinking about it either, but of course she had no control over that. It was weeks before she felt again the insouciance that had been dissipated by Detective Noonan's phone call.

Of course he must remember her. That was scarcely two years ago. She decided that he was being gallant, that his silence was a sign of respect for her. She had come up in the world since, and that could explain it too. Nor could it be ruled out that he had forgotten, of course, but she really didn't believe that was possible.

One morning he showed up at the office with some astonishing information.

"Ambrose Hennessy came downtown to tell us that he murdered Lilian Dahl."

"No!"

"He had a very elaborate story and didn't like it when Manfredi gave him the bum's rush."

She looked at him. "Because he was making it up?"

"According to him, he had a big thing going with Lilian Dahl, and when she tried to end it he got angry and killed her."

"There is good reason to think there was an affair . . ." Virginia stopped, shut her eyes, waved her hand in front of her face as if to erase thoughts from her mind. Then she looked sadly at Noonan. "Why would he do such a thing? And now?"

"Rachel Salma showed up to confess the same day."

"Confess that she had killed Lilian?"

Whatever reception Ambrose's confession might have received in its own right, it had been rendered farcical by Rachel's claim to have done the same thing.

"They should have coordinated their stories," Virginia said.

"Maybe they did."

"It certainly doesn't sound like it."

"It isn't supposed to. Imagine he's telling the truth."

"How could he be? You've seen how he reveres her memory. They all do, of course, but Ambrose even more so."

"When you say there is evidence of something going on between Ambrose and Lilian, I suppose you mean in these papers."

"Yes . . ." Virginia stopped. Things had to be interpreted, the allusions were oblique.

"Like the poem whose initial letters spelled Ambrose M?"

Captain Manfredi had discovered that, so of course Noonan was not likely to think that hints and allusions were beyond their power.

"Look. Let's stipulate that Ambrose and the poet were having an affair." On that supposition, Ambrose's story that he had gone into a rage when told it was all over has a foundation. Say the whole story was true. "Okay. Now add to that his fear that reopening the investigation would finally find the truth of what happened."

"He's so afraid he confesses?"

"But not until he and Rachel work out a way in which he can immunize himself precisely by confessing."

"She confesses the same thing?"

"But independently. As if neither knew what the other was doing. Of course Manfredi laughs the two of them out of the office. Now he's sorry we opened it up again, to the degree that we have."

"I suppose it does seem silly from a policeman's point of view to be wondering about her death after all these years."

"There's no statute of limitations on murder."

103

"Did he say what he did with the body?"

"He buried it in a greenhouse."

"A greenhouse!"

"Rachel Salma said she put the body in a garment bag, weighted it by zipping a concrete block into the bag and dumped it in the river."

"Rachel did all that." Virginia was laughing.

"You see. It's a joke. Of course the body would have been discovered, nine times out of ten. So his story is taken to be equally ridiculous."

"What are you going to do?"

"I don't like the thought that we would just drop it. Re-opening an investigation after all these years more or less out of curiosity is pretty hard to justify. But we did start looking into it and now we get these confessions. Do me a favor."

"What?"

"Let me see some of the evidence that Ambrose Hennessy and Lilian Dahl were having an affair."

"I'll need a little time."

He shrugged. "It's already been thirty years."

His tenacity was unnerving. Had he pursued the spoor of her connection with Chip? Had he believed her story about the key? She did not like the prospect of all that professional curiosity being turned on these papers. She was connected with them now and that made her feel vulnerable to Noonan's curiosity.

She decided that she would provide him with only the most equivocal and dubious passages from the papers.

Manfredi

1

Noonan said he hadn't mentioned to the new Mrs. Basil Bauer her connection with the death of the late Chip Bufalo.

"Why would you?" Manfredi said. "That was two years ago!"

"Not as fresh as a missing person report thirty years old?"

"Look, she lived in the building where the guy went out his kitchen window on the fifth floor."

"Lots of people lived there. She live on the fifth floor?"

"The third."

"You remembered that."

"I interviewed her at the time. Back when I was a cop and we followed up all kind of suggestions, most of them worthless. We interviewed everybody and most people will say something you might want to look into."

"Like, this person was close to the deceased."

"Yes."

"This person being Virginia Hardie."

"That's right."

"And you asked her about that?"

"Of course I did."

"When you've talked to her lately, has she mentioned those earlier discussions?"

"No."

"She hasn't."

"Neither have I."

"Why not?"

Noonan decided to shut up. Was he on trial or something? Manfredi shrugged. He turned over sheets of paper in the folder before him. "I see a key to her apartment was found on the suicide."

"I didn't realize that until some time later. I thought he had two keys to his own place. When I tried to open the door with one of them, I found out different. One key was to her place."

"Virginia Hardie's."

"Yes."

"And you asked her about it."

"She had given him a key so he could get in to water her plants while she was away."

Manfredi said nothing. He sat motionless. The big wind-up watch he'd had all his life lay on the desk, its ticking audible. He looked up at Noonan.

"If you were me and I were you, what would you think of this bullshit?"

"Tell me."

"You couldn't wait to reopen the investigation into the fate of a woman who has been missing thirty years. You're not much over thirty so you know that's a long time. But here we have an alleged suicide with an unusual woman on the premises, the key to whose apartment is on the dead man's body, and I don't have the coroner's report. There was an autopsy certainly?"

"You want the coroner's report."

"And after you bring it to me I want you to go out and have a good talk with Virginia Hardie. Not as a friend, not as your guide in wondering about Lilian Dahl, but as someone who has some explaining to do in the death of Chip Bufalo."

"What case are we reopening?"

"Get out of here."

Manfredi had been around long enough to know that we bawl out other people when we know we ourselves have goofed. He had been caught up in the romance of Lilian Dahl's disappearance every bit as much as Noonan had. Noonan had not been assigned to him at the time of the investigation into the death of Chip Bufalo, but it was Noonan who drew his attention to the newspaper photograph with Virginia in it, and he had also provided the newspaper clips quoting her. Maybe it meant nothing, but that isn't something you just assume. Alarms should have gone off in his head at that point. He should have demanded a good look at Virginia Hardie. They were relying on her too much already in the Lilian Dahl matter.

Manfredi wanted to be a lot clearer on the death of Chip Bufalo, which had occurred only two years ago, before he got excited about a poet disappearing decades ago.

2

The Bufalo autopsy report was a revelation. The coroner drew attention to contusions on the head that did not seem accounted for by the fact that the deceased had landed on his chest. The neck had snapped as the head was subjected to two powerful forces, one downward, the other upward, caused by the impact. The nose had been smashed and the forehead all but flattened. This did not account for the signs that the deceased had suffered severe damage to the back of the head. The contusions made one think of blows. There was the possibility that these had been inflicted during the downward descent, but they had been suffered at roughly the same time as the other damage to the body and the instant death it had effected.

That was one thing. The other was the description of the room from which the deceased had begun his fall. The first officers on the scene said the kitchen looked like a mess. There were prints from the deceased's shoes all over the floor, black marks made by the soles of his shoes. No account was attempted of these facts. Manfredi wondered if the scene didn't suggest a struggle, even an assailant.

"We considered that possibility," Noonan said.

"And ruled it out."

"There were no marks made by any shoes other than Chip Bufalo's." Noonan tried to keep the triumph out of his tone.

"The floor wasn't dusted."

"Dusted! For what?"

"Footprints."

"Geez. We dusted every surface."

"I see that. Prints other than those of the deceased were found."

"Old prints."

"Left by people watering his plants?"

"Do you want me to get a set of prints from Virginia?"

"If it won't destroy your friendship."

3

His own big mistake had been too much buddy buddy business with Noonan. He had forgotten that he was the oldest active member of the force, that he had earned a reputation for steady adherence to routine, forget the fancy theories. The number of murders that required a fancy theory was less than five, maybe less than two percent. As often as not, the investigating officer began with knowledge of who had committed the crime. The task was to present to the prosecutor evidence that could not be dismissed on some technicality, thereby getting the guilty person off scot-free.

They had two events now when arguably no crime had been committed. One person walks away, disappears into thin air, another takes a dive out his kitchen window, an unassisted suicide. Suicide was still against the law and anyone threatening it or attempting it would be stopped. Manfredi suspected that the rationale for the illegality, even criminality, of suicide had been lost. The country was different than it had been. For some time there had been people agitating for the right to kill themselves. Now the argument was that they had a right to be killed by a doctor, in antiseptic circumstances, with the full sanction of the law. Manfredi didn't like it. He knew it was wrong.

But nothing like that was involved in Chip Bufalo's going out his window. If his suicide had been assisted, then it wasn't suicide. If someone whacked him on the head a couple times before helping him out the window, that someone ought to be prosecuted. Maybe the physical evidence did not support the judgment that Chip Bufalo had been killed by someone other than himself, but Manfredi was ashamed of the fact that they had not pursued the matter when the coroner's report came in.

It eased his mind some when he checked back and remembered how overwhelmed the department had been at the time. There had been the Rollo phenomenon. Rollo Cortez had parked in front of headquarters and come in to say he had killed fifteen, maybe sixteen women. Why should they believe him? He had one outside in the trunk of his car. He had been on his way to dispose of the body when he thought better of it and stopped in, wanting to have his career cut short.

The manpower needed to check out Rollo's recollections of when and who and where had been enormous. Public relations had to hire people to handle the media. Other jurisdictions hoped Rollo could clear up still open cases of missing women.

Nor was that all. A woman found her daughter performing acts of witchcraft in her room, checked it out and found that diabolism was rife in her daughter's high school. The circle had kidnapped a baby from a stroller in the mall and had a ritual killing.

And so on. No excuses, but still there were mitigating circumstances. And Noonan had been a young detective on whose shoulders the Chip Bufalo death had been placed. Everybody else was busy. But now they had a chance to clear it up, and by God that is what Manfredi wanted done.

Walking out of your life without saying goodbye was not a criminal act—so long as you owed no money, had no obligations to children and relatives, and weren't fleeing to avoid facing the music for some crime. Police spent a lot of time on missing persons reports, not because the one missing was a fugitive, though sometimes that happened, but because the ones left behind were frantic to learn what had happened. Alzheimer cases apart and amnesiacs, the thing about a missing person was that he knew where he was. Maybe there was just a powerful desire no longer to be oneself. In that it was like suicide. But with the difference that life went on, only different and better than before. A third of the time, the missing person was with another missing person of the opposite sex, so maybe bigamy was involved. But there were pure cases of disappearance. No apparent motive, no prior attempts, as was often the case in a successful suicide, and no clues. Hard on those abandoned, a nuisance to the police, but no crime.

Had Chip Bufalo been a suicide?

Had Lilian Dahl been a pure case of disappearance?

Were the two linked via Virginia Hardie?

4

"I feel like a girl who offers her body and is refused." Ambrose Hennessy smiled ruefully. "It is not every day that one admits to having committed murder and is sent on his way like a nuisance."

"I had to make way for the next penitent."

"Ah, Rachel. A pathetic but withal noble attempt to save me. I am surprised that Alma hasn't confessed as well. But I of course have proof."

"The body."

"The *corpus delicti* or, I might add, the *mulier delecta*."

"What does that mean?"

Hennessy grew grave. "Captain, I am not trying to be Walter Mitty."

"Who is he?"

"You really don't know?"

"No."

"I think you do and that you have adopted the policy to discount, disbelieve and dismiss anything I say."

"Professor Salma says she threw the body in the river."

"Patently absurd. But that is her purpose. She is trumping me—"

"Why?"

"To save me."

"You're in no danger."

"You don't intend to listen carefully to the details of what happened and to take steps to verify or falsify what I say?"

"Not at this time."

Hennessy sat back with a theatrical sigh. "I can scarcely plead urgency, after concealing the matter all these years."

"Have you told Basil Bauer?"

"I am ashamed to face him. Twice I have stood at his side when he married. The best man. My God. I lusted after his first wife and I lust after this one."

"She is attractive. How well do you know her?"

"In the circumstances, that is a leading question."

"I mean it in the usual sense. How long have you known her?"

"You're serious."

"Yes."

"I have known her for something over two years, three years. When she became a graduate student."

"But you're retired."

"Only recently. I had intended to stay on until I was carried out in a box, but a time comes when one sees that a graceful exit is still just possible."

"You could have gone on?"

"Until I was drooling out of both corners of my mouth. It is now considered an assault on one's constitutional rights to suggest that age takes its toll on mind and body. Each of us is a featureless unit before the law, without age or gender—with exceptions—family, talents, understanding. The years pass but they leave the essential self untouched."

"I am the senior person on the force."

"Are you? I would never have guessed. I myself was the dean of the faculty when I retired, meaning the senior active member. Do you take pride in your status?"

Manfredi shrugged.

"Of course you do. It is pardonable pride, perhaps, at least to a point. You are far from reaching that point. I very nearly passed it."

"You're content doing nothing?"

"I would be content if I could do nothing. But one's life continues to be regulated. Theoretically I could sleep all day if I want to, but I would have to answer to the housekeeping staff. If I eat in, it is at a stated time. And there are doctors to see, and lawyers, a veritable round of appointments. Nothing? Nothing is what God created the world from and it hasn't existed since."

Grudgingly Manfredi conceded that Ambrose Hennessy was an agreeable old fart. Full of blarney like other Irishmen Manfredi had known, but there was style in his grumbling and art in his complaints. Hennessy could make his boredom seem exciting. But it was apparently not exciting enough to him.

"A murder confession should liven up your life."

Hennessy shook his head slowly. "Of course you would say that. We are all psychiatrists now. Would you want me to analyze you?"

Manfredi knew a moment's panic. Hennessy had sat forward as he asked the question, and seemed eager to begin.

"Not on the public's time."

"Ah. I am glad you brought that up. It must be annoying to have every drunk and rascal tell you that he pays your salary and you work for him. I will only interpret your remark as descriptive of your employment by the people. It is in your capacity as servant of the public that I have come back to you, Captain. It is not pleasant to be treated like a recalcitrant schoolboy who won't stop pestering you. It would be overly dramatic to say that I demand that you verify what I have said, but I do expect it."

"I will give it every consideration."

Hennessy sat in silence for a moment. "Well?"

"I have said . . ."

"Then you must ask me questions. You must ask me the circumstances, you must ask me precisely where I buried the body."

"In a greenhouse."

"A very particular greenhouse. It is attached to the garage of the house that Basil and Lilian lived in on Collier Avenue."

Manfredi wrote it down. He must not act as if he was humoring Hennessy, but he had to get him out of here. Maxwell, who had worked with Noonan on the Chip Bufalo death, was due in ten minutes.

Seven minutes later, Hennessy stood, partially placated at least. On the sheet before him, Manfredi had made a list of the major points in Hennessy's confession.

"I would start with the greenhouse."

"I'll be in touch."

"You will indeed."

5

There are athletes and actors who shave their heads in order to achieve the condition that had come to Mark Maxwell naturally. And early. He was bald in the class picture when he graduated from the police academy. And he was bald twenty-three years later, skin bald. A well-shaped head can neutralize the effect of baldness. Maxwell's head looked the way an elbow in the ribs feels. And it made you want to look away, as unattractive nakedness does. Manfredi felt like asking Maxwell to put his hat back on.

"God, this building brings it all back."

"Getting sentimental?"

"I hate this place. I hate the smell of it, the look of it, the sounds. How can you stand it?"

"Actually I do a lot of sitting."

There was the sound of escaping air. Maxwell's shoulders lifted, his eyes widened. He was laughing.

"I just finished my run." Maxwell wore chinos and a baggy

sweatshirt that was earning its name and huge white tennis shoes that made embarrassing noises on the uncarpeted floor. "I run every day. The doctor says I have the heart of a teen-ager."

"Transplants are a marvelous thing."

Again, escaping air as the shoulders lifted and the eyes widened. "Maybe you remember my first marathon."

Maxwell had come in third in the local marathon in his first years as a cop. It had given him a purpose in life. He ran every year after that, but had never again done so well. In retirement he devoted himself to running. He intended to win the local marathon, go on to others, make a kind of career of it.

"I'm glad I caught you now then. You were involved in the investigation of the death of Chip Bufalo."

Maxwell sat very still for half a minute and then began to bob his head. "Guy went out a window?"

"That's the one. You didn't say the guy who jumped out a window."

"Do we know that for sure now?"

"The coroner said possible suicide."

"Have you talked with him?"

"Foss? He's dead. Do you have his number?"

Escaping air. Maxwell made laughter sound worse than a death rattle.

"Didn't he put his doubts in his report? If we'd had the time, we'd have kept on it."

"You think he was pushed?"

"People in the building thought he was pushed."

"Why?"

"He had been run out of Pocatello. He couldn't get in front of the camera again. He had enemies."

"Like?"

"You want their names?"

"How about those in the building who voiced suspicion."

"There was one old bag who wanted to tell me about the guy's sex life. Not that she knew anything about it. But she was sure someone was having fun and she didn't like it. Look at what happened. If that is all there was, I mean besides what Foss found, fine, scrub it, we're busy."

"You figure it was just gossip."

"You know about the keys?"

"Tell me about that."

Maxwell shifted in his chair. He needed a shower, but then he had run ten miles to get here.

"A young guy named Noonan discovered that one of the keys found on the body wasn't to his apartment. Same key, wrong door."

"Did you talk to the lady whose door it fit?"

Maxwell squeezed more laughter from his lungs. "We're thinking a lover's quarrel, she gets real mad and flips him out the window. This woman was petite! She couldn't throw herself out a window."

"But the contusions on the back of the head?"

"That took her out of it even more. Chip Bufalo weighed more than two hundred pounds. The lady about a hundred. How many people do you know can lift twice their weight? No, the key might have meant only what she said. They looked after each other's place when one was gone."

"You check to see if either of them was away much?"

Maxwell shook his head. "That was a dead alley. I wanted to check out everyone at the studio. I wanted us to get in touch with Pocatello. None of that happened. You remember how busy we were."

He offered to take Maxwell down to the cafeteria for a cup of coffee.

"Coffee! I haven't had a cup of coffee in years."

"What do you drink?"

"Mineral water."

"Maybe they have mineral water."

"I gotta go. If that's it? Good. I'm going to run home as well. Not quite a marathon, but it will have to do."

"Until the real thing comes along."

"You remember that song."

"If I could sing I would sing it."

Maxwell struck a pose, closed his eyes and sang the song. Like an angel. He had a beautiful voice. He might have made a living with it if he could have done something about his head. Manfredi tried to join in, but Maxwell opened his eyes in pain at the sound of it so he shut up.

6

He told Noonan about his conversation with Maxwell.

"Thanks for the vote of confidence. I would have liked to hear what he had to say."

"He's got quite a memory."

"Well, what did I forget?"

"How many people do you know who can lift twice their own weight?"

"I have to stand up twice to do it."

"Do you remember Maxwell's laugh?"

"The slow leak?" Noonan made a face. "He was a slow leak too. Stop at a McDonald's he was into the john like a shot. You could have a whole cup of coffee before he came out. I told him he would get arrested for loitering."

"Maybe he had kidney stones."

"He had rocks in his head. Wouldn't drink coffee. You ever been to McDonald's with a guy who asks for tea?"

"Or mineral water."

"Right. He can't drink soft drinks. He wants to provide an on-the-spot chemical analysis to those at the counter. A real spur to business. But he was a great cop."

"He doesn't think it was suicide."

"The coroner did."

"Possible suicide."

"That's not like impossible suicide. He also said that he had never had a body that didn't present unanswerable questions as to how it got that way."

"He said that?"

"Here is a guy falls five floors and hits the pavement with a splat. Did he fall or did he jump? How do you accidentally fall out a window in the middle of the night? I made the mistake of asking the coroner. He went on and on."

"With contusions all over your head."

"He had a dozen possible explanations for those."

"Possible."

"Conceivable."

The conversation had begun on a strained note, became friendly and now was getting edgy again. Manfredi could understand why Noonan would not enjoy being second-guessed and his work criticized, but it all made Manfredi's point. If a two-year-old fall out a window had this many question marks, how could they expect to come up with a plausible explanation of a woman disappearing thirty years after the fact?

"I had a nice talk with Hennessy about his confession."

"Did he take it back?"

"On the contrary."

"How does he explain Rachel Salma?"

"Gallantry. She is trying to save him by negating his confession with a patently absurd one."

"Are we dropping it?"

"Not yet. I told Alma I'd talk to her and I want to do that. And I want to ask Basil about his greenhouse."

"I didn't know he had one."

"He doesn't now. It's at the house in which he and Lilian lived and where he stayed until his retirement. Out on Collier."

"Potted poet?"

Manfredi did an imitation of Maxwell's laugh and sounded like a whoopie cushion.

Becoming enamored of elderly women is probably a perversion with a name of its own, but the experience was new to Manfredi. Most old women struck him the way Rachel Salma did, but Alma was something else. She was pert and she was cute and had girlish mannerisms; moreover she dressed the part. Once it would have been rare for a woman to live to her age—or for a man, for that matter—but to live that long with so little sign of wear and tear was a phenomenon. He couldn't stop himself from mentioning it when they were seated in her living room.

"Oh it runs in the family." She stopped and adopted a naughty expression. "My daddy used to say that noses run in our family."

"How old did he get?"

"He's still alive. My mother too."

"They're in good shape?"

"Their hobby is ballroom dancing."

"I suppose having both your parents alive helps."

"Helps what?"

"Feeling young?"

"Believe me I'm only laughing on the outside."

"But crying on the inside?"

She began to hum. She asked if he would like to see her collection of golden oldies. She put on an old 78, Sinatra

119

when his voice was perfect, and the music drove the present from the room.

"Do you dance?"

They danced. Manfredi could not believe this. Here was this little knockout, seventy-two years old, and he had her in his arms, dancing to Hugo Winterhalter's orchestra and Frankie on the vocal. She followed it with Dick Haymes.

"Just one. He had such a voice. If I had to run away with one of them, I really think it would have been with Dick Haymes."

She began to hum and Manfredi found himself envying Dick Haymes—not for his voice but because he had won Alma's heart.

"If you had stayed longer at Basil and his bride's reception, you would have heard nothing but songs like this. I supplied the deejay with records. Actually, he made a tape of the whole program. You might be able to get a copy of it."

"It sounds illegal."

"So is the music business."

He told her that Ambrose Hennessy had confessed to the murder of Lilian Dahl.

"It would have made more sense if he had killed Basil."

"Do you think he killed her?"

"Why would he say so if he didn't?"

This was a surprise. Manfredi had been prepared to meet a solid wall of protective friends who would assure him that Ambrose Hennessy had been incapable of such a thing.

"Why would he kill Basil?"

"If he were going to kill anyone, is what I meant."

"He was jealous of Basil."

"Now, Captain, don't do that. The trouble with looking like Betty Boop is that people think you haven't a brain in your head."

"Who said you looked like Betty Boop?"

"Lilian. Or so I'm told. Will the police be privy to all those papers?"

"If we have to wait until someone has gone through all those papers, all of us will be dead."

"The more I think of it, the more I believe Lilian's disappearance has its roots in Ambrose's and Basil's childhood. I am not being Freudian. I mean when they were in school together. The school has ceased to exist and nobody knew of it when it did, but those two speak of it as if it were a combination of Eton, Choate and the Jesuit *ratio studiorum*."

"What's that?"

"It doesn't matter. Their memories have so inflated the school and the time they spent there that it exceeds all possible comparisons. No doubt it opened the minds of two boys from lower-middle class homes and gave them a good grounding in the classics and a genuine love of literature. Has either of them spoken to you about their school?"

"No."

"I would urge you to get them talking about the place. Separately. One of them is bad enough on the subject, but as a duet they are beyond belief."

"This would be like high school?"

"Like and unlike. But those are the years."

"When the twig was bent?"

"It is deeper than that. It was then that they defined themselves in terms of one another. I am not a fatalist save in the sense that I believe we freely create our fates. I am told this is logical nonsense, but it is the only view that makes sense. Take yourself."

"Please."

She wrinkled her nose in incomprehension.

"Henny Youngman."

"Oh, that dreadful man. When he died the papers treated his jokes as if they were the epigrams of Martial. A man says to a lawyer, Can I ask you two questions. Lawyer: what's the second question." She began to laugh in the middle of the joke.

"You remembered that."

"Trying to rid the mind of them once heard is the difficulty."

"You were going to take me."

"Now don't get your hopes up, young man. I was explaining fate. You are a policeman. There was a time when you could have become something else."

"A mailman."

"A hundred other things. You freely chose to become a policeman. But once you have become a policeman, you are confined and restricted, things are expected of you, by yourself and others. You are no longer free."

"I could retire."

"Don't! It is awful."

"And Basil and Ambrose have the fate they chose as boys."

She brought a finger to the tip of her pretty nose. "I take back what I said, about killing Basil rather than Lilian. That's not true. Ambrose and Basil go way back, Lilian was a comparative newcomer. If Ambrose was jealous of Basil, killing Basil in order to have Lilian would have deprived him of the one audience he cared about, the audience of one."

"Basil?"

"Basil."

7

"He is being childish and I told him so." Basil spoke with the tolerance of a parent. "He might have known that would stir Rachel to do something."

"I wonder if the two of them didn't plan it."

"Plan that they would both lay claim to killing Lilian? Perhaps, perhaps. What shocks and dismays me is that it is Lilian they are speaking of. Granted, many years have passed and she has acquired mythical status among us, but even so, to talk of killing her is cruel and heartless."

"And then the way they claimed to have gotten rid of the body."

Basil lost his censorious expression. "What did they say?"

"Rachel threw the body off a bridge."

"Good heavens."

"Ambrose says he buried the body in your greenhouse."

"My greenhouse. Oh, that is truly childish."

"How so?"

"He always resented my Churchill phase."

Under the influence of the great prime minister, Basil had first tried to paint, but his lack of talent drew so many rebukes he sought another way to emulate the great man. During his inactive years, politically, Churchill had worked on his estate, improving the grounds and he himself constructed a brick wall.

"He was quite lyrical about the pleasures of laying bricks. I can attest to it from my own experience. At our home on Collier Avenue, I learned to lay bricks by building a wall along the back of the property. It was addictive. When I added the greenhouse to the garage, I did everything myself except, of course, the glazing. But the excavation and walling it with brick and bringing that wall two feet above ground level, I did that. I even made a brick floor for the greenhouse. No mortar, the bricks laid in patterns and embedded in sand. When it was finished, I'd had my fill of bricklaying. Throughout, Ambrose was mocking and caustic. Something of this must lie behind his claim to have buried Lilian there." Suddenly he shivered. "I cannot believe that we would ever speak of her like this."

"You two were in school together, weren't you."

Basil's manner was immediately altered, and he spoke with the delight that Alma had prepared Manfredi for. "Ambrose is my oldest friend. We were thirteen years old when we first met. That is nearly sixty years ago."

Manfredi calculated that the beloved wife had only been gone half that time. Basil was speaking of the truly formative years of one's life, the friends, the reading, the place. He was off and running, as Alma had warned. As mere boys they composed poetry, in Latin as well as English. Their lives revolved around *Quid Nunc*, the student publication. In their senior year they had served as joint editors of *Quid Nunc*, neither wanting the job at the expense of the other.

"We began a novel, I would write a chapter, he would write the next. It got bigger and bigger. We never finished it. It appeared in installments in *Quid Nunc* and when we graduated it just stopped."

"You never finished it?"

"No, we never did."

"Do you have copies of *Quid Nunc*?"

"Of course. I had them bound eventually. Ambrose has a set as well. All our juvenilia."

"It sounds like a golden age."

"That's just what it was!" Suddenly Basil began to speak in a way unintelligible to Manfredi. He went on for minutes, then smiled. "The opening lines of the *Odyssey*."

"That's pretty impressive."

"Both Basil and Ambrose are Greek names."

"You can recite lots of Greek?"

"And Latin. Memorization comes easily when you're young.

You never really lose what you commit to memory then."

"Do you think Ambrose could have killed your wife?"

"Oh yes."

"You do!"

"I sometimes thought of killing her myself. Seriously. She was so perfect. And then I would think of her growing old, perhaps losing her gift, poets sometimes do. A Keatsian thought."

"The Grecian Urn?"

"You know it? Bravo. Ambrose has Keats by the yard. He recites much better than I do."

"How would you have killed her?"

"I will tell you a secret. During the dreadful days immediately following her disappearance, I half-convinced myself that I had killed her . . ."

Manfredi tuned him out and got ready to leave. How slyly Basil had entered a third bid for the death of his wife. She was legally dead, having been gone so long, but there was no proof that she had died. Yet three people, two dear friends and now in a way her husband, were claiming to have killed her. The waters into which Rachel had not thrown the dead body of Lilian Dahl were muddied indeed by these competing, absurd claims to have murdered her.

Why were the three of them doing this? Clearly, they did not want a police investigation of the disappearance of Lilian Dahl. The woman had acquired mythical status and it better served the purposes of their remembering that her going be shrouded in mystery.

8

Manfredi now saw Virginia in a new light. The contrast between the young graduate student, living in an apartment and sharing keys with a one-time television star from Pocatello, and the new Mrs. Basil Bauer, custodian of the papers and reputation of the first Mrs. Bauer, the poet Lilian Dahl, whose reputation had gained rather than suffered from the fact that one day she disappeared, could not have been greater. In the first setting, she had a brush with death, when Chip Bufalo went out his kitchen window. Before writing finis to the whole business, Manfredi went out to see Virginia.

"I hope you're not expecting those references this soon."

Manfredi waved his hand and took the chair she offered. "I think I have been outsmarted by your friends."

She smiled.

"But what's the surprise? They were all college teachers; I'm just a dumb cop."

"Uh huh."

"About Chip." Her manner had been a little condescending, borrowed from her friends, but she stiffened at the mention of the dead television writer. "Since you knew him better than anyone else in that building, you must have had some idea what really happened to him."

She sighed. "This is becoming something very much like harassment."

"I am sorry you feel that way. When he died, the department was busier than it normally is, and other pressing matters left an unsatisfying resolution of the investigation."

"And now you have time on your hands?"

With Alma, he might have sung, or tried to sing, "And you on my mind." But that would have given credence to a complaint of harassment of another kind.

"Even refugees from Pocatello deserve a fair shake."

"I have no idea what happened to him."

"He never mentioned feeling threatened?"

"Captain Manfredi, he committed suicide. That was the resolution of the investigation. Why do you find it so hard to accept?"

When he went to see her it was with the vague idea of talking about her new associates. He had come to tell her things, not to ask them, and it was the present not the past that was on his mind. He was tired of the past. Talking with Alma, with Ambrose and Rachel, with Basil her new husband, he got the sense of a vast network of remembered events that did not include Virginia, yet she was now positioned in their very midst. What would he have said if he tried to say it?

He asked himself that, driving back to his office. On the radio came something alleged to be music. He turned it off. He rolled down the window on the passenger side and let the world and its noise come at him live.

A mile farther on, he called in to ask Noonan to go to lunch with him, but Gloria reminded him that this was Noonan's day off.

Friday came and then the weekend and a parish banquet for the retiring pastor, Monsignor Luke "Bingo" Blanchette. The priest associated Manfredi with recurrent efforts to shut down parish bingo, but this was compensated for by the piety of Mrs. Manfredi. He missed most of the first game but bought a card and settled down to enjoy the second from start to finish. Later, when his wife became engrossed in one of the phony police dramas on television, Manfredi turned in early.

Noonan came into his office before he got settled in.

"Basil Bauer called to say his wife is missing. He hasn't seen her for three days."

Manfredi sat in silence through this, noting the slightly accusing tone with which it was said.

"Do you believe him?"

"I'm going to check it out."

"Keep me posted."

Noonan left. Gloria brought him coffee. He leafed through the morning paper and then set it aside. Sipping his coffee he looked out the window. Is this how it began thirty years ago? He rotated his chair and shouted at Gloria.

"Tell Noonan to get back in here!"

Part Two

Manfredi

1

"I want recorded statements from everyone."

"Everyone."

"You start with Basil. He made the call?"

"Yes."

"Himself? It wasn't someone calling for him?"

"I'll check."

"Do that."

Noonan's jaw firmed and he ground his teeth. He actually jumped when Manfredi shouted.

"Gloria! Get in here. I want minutes taken of this meeting."

This time, by God, an investigation was going to be conducted according to the book. Noonan, and to some extent Manfredi himself, had apparently become a diversion for the retired members of the Fort Elbow faculty who resided at the Residenza. When things get boring, call up the police and confess to a crime. Well by God, from now on they were going to be made to see the seriousness of enlisting the police in whatever game they were playing.

Gloria came in with her eyebrows far above her glasses and her eyes framed in lots of white. She was carrying her book and settled into a chair.

"Ready."

"Subject. Alleged disappearance of Virginia Bauer."

"You're kidding." The dentist who had convinced Gloria

to edge those eye teeth with gold ought to be shot. This was Gloria's first knowledge of the call about Virginia. Manfredi had told Noonan to get the hell down to his office and in the meantime he had tried to see his way clear on this. He could ignore the call entirely, and be subject to censure, though he thought he could carry the board with him when he gave them an account of recent events. He could set in motion a slow-motion half-assed search that would be tantamount to ignoring the call but technically a response to it. Or he could do what he decided to do, pursue this thing absolutely by the book with as little influence as was humanly possible of the events of recent weeks when he and Noonan had come to know the principals.

But Noonan was of another mind. As soon as Gloria was ready he said he wanted to make a statement.

"I want it on the record that there is good reason to think that the person reported missing may have been reacting to what she regarded as harassment by this office."

Gloria's pencil slowed in the course of writing this down, but she kept her eyes on the page after she was done.

"Is that your phrase or hers?"

"Harassment? Hers."

"By which she is referring to efforts by this office to ask some questions about the death of Chip Bufalo, which should have been asked and pursued two years ago. You're saying she fled rather than answer questions about that death?"

"Who the hell do you think you are, Manfredi, the bureau of standards? You're on the shelf, don't you see that? Why I've been assigned here I don't know."

"Perhaps to learn how to conduct an investigation."

"An investigation! This is a missing person's report. Let old Manfredi handle it. He won't retire and he's got to do something."

"You're saying the call is a ruse?"

"Would you like to hear some statistics on missing persons? I looked them up."

"Already? You should have asked me. Gloria could have given you the data I collected weeks ago."

"I'll get them," Gloria said.

"Forget it," Noonan said.

Gloria looked at Manfredi. Good girl. She knew who she worked for. "Maybe you'd better leave us alone, Gloria."

She was out of there in record time, pulling the door closed behind her.

"Noonan, if you think working on this case is beneath your dignity, I'll have you reassigned."

"My assignment does not depend upon you."

"If you mean I can't fire you, you're right. But if I ask to have you transferred . . ."

"You'll make your day. Old Manfredi at it again. Maybe they'll ask you to come down and tell them about how it used it be."

"Or you could ask for reassignment yourself."

"Not on your life. Seeing the way you've screwed things up already, I think I owe it to the department to stick around and keep you under control."

"That's decent of you. Are you through?"

"That's a question I don't have to put to you."

"That's right. Do you understand your assignment?"

Noonan stood. "Written statements from everyone."

"Go to it."

Noonan's face was red, his hands were fists, and his mouth trembled in anger at his inability to elicit from Manfredi any visible emotion.

Noonan slammed the door when he left, adding that mistake to his others. Not that his word had not gone home. It was an old trick familiar from marital disputes to invoke the negative judgments of unnamed others to bolster one's accusation. Manfredi understood that. At the same time he had a vivid image of young colleagues chuckling about things he did or said. He did talk a lot about the past, the way it had been, as if once there had been a golden age and now there was now. Maybe he had stayed on too long.

That was something he could brood about later. It was Noonan's initial accusation that rang true, not about harassment, but that Virginia had felt the heat of the reopening of the inquiry into the death of Chip Bufalo and decided to go. But such a departure could only make sense if she were directly involved in his death and felt that this was bound to come out. Noonan had spoken as if coming to the defense of a lady, but he apparently had not thought through what he was saying. The logical consequence of his explanation would be to regard Virginia as a fugitive, not just a missing person.

2

Ambrose Hennessy smiled tentatively and leaned closer to Manfredi. "I thought I heard you say that Virginia is missing."

"You hadn't already heard?"

"Hadn't heard! Of course not. Who says this? Who called you?"

"The caller said he was Basil Bauer."

"It couldn't have been."

"Detective Noonan is with him now."

"Missing? For how long?"

"Three days."

"Impossible! I had dinner with Basil last night."

"Just Basil?"

"No, no. Everyone was here. Old McMullin celebrated his ninetieth birthday."

"Basil came here to the Residenza?"

"He and McMullin are like that." He crossed two arthritic fingers, wincing as he did.

"But he came alone, without his wife?"

"Virginia didn't know McMullin. You should know that it is always reassuring to have someone even older than oneself." But Hennessy called himself to order. "Basil said nothing about Virginia. There has to be a mistake."

"Do you suppose someone is playing a joke?"

"If they are, I hope you hang them."

"Again, for the record. This is the first you have heard of the disappearance of Virginia?"

"My God, just the sound of that."

"Yes or no."

"Yes. Yes, this is the first I've heard of it. I must call Basil."

Alma put back her head and laughed. "You're pulling my leg."

Last time they talked he would have responded facetiously to that, but today was different. Alma's expression altered as she studied him.

"You're serious."

"We received a call to that effect."

"When?"

"The call came this morning. The message was that she had not been seen for three days. Of course we must check it out."

"Three days."

"Yes."

"It has to be a hoax. Basil was here with us last night. He

135

said nothing about a disappearance."

"How did he act?"

"Basilesque. He was in rare form. He recited Catullus's poem to his brother, the one that ends *ave atque vale*. Fortunately McMullin didn't remember that the brother was dead."

"But Virginia wasn't with him?"

"With all us old folks?" A flirty little smile, inviting him to exempt her from the class of old folks. She was humming *Autumn Leaves*.

"You can tell me nothing that might have indicated this might happen?"

"But what exactly has happened?"

Rachel Salma was not surprised. "I've said from the beginning she isn't just interested in Lilian, she wants to *be* her. She comes to Fort Elbow to study, not exactly the Athens of our times. Her sole interest was Lilian's association with the campus. I suppose she discovered that Basil, although retired, was still alive, still seeing students on a special basis, so that put him in the target area. He had actually been married to Lilian! Well you can see the next step."

"She marries Basil."

"Who cannot plead ignorance. I laid it all out for him. She became a wedge between us all from the beginning. It wasn't the same. She was always so *there*. She wanted to be Basil's keeper, she wanted control of those papers. Well, she got it. She married him and moved him out of here and away from all his friends. He was here last night, by the way. I hadn't seen him so happy since the day he got married. That was here, too, of course. But then she took him away, rented an office."

"So what do you make of the disappearance?"

"How long is she supposed to have been missing?"

"Three days."

Another derisive laugh. "It's part of the picture. Lilian disappeared so she will disappear. Not for good, alas, what would be the point? No, she will stay out of sight sufficiently long for there to be maximum publicity and then she will return with some dramatic story."

"I hope you're right."

"Can't you bring charges against someone for turning in a false report?"

"You mean against Basil?"

"Did Basil make the call?"

That was twice. The call had been made on 911 so it was recorded, but it might have been coming from the moon. Man or woman, who could say? Manfredi wouldn't have bet much that it was Basil's voice, or that it wasn't. He was almost surprised when the caller, when asked, identified himself as Basil Bauer.

3

When he came in the next morning there was a report from Noonan on his desk.

"I wish you two would make up," Gloria said.

"He had to blow off a little steam."

"You were really going at him."

"I thought I was the soul of reason."

"That's what I mean."

Noonan's report was on his interview with Basil Bauer.

Basil

1

Was it Goethe who said that things happen the first time as tragedy and the second time as farce? Something like that, but it was more likely Hegel. Basil shook his head to rid it of such footnotes. He was annoyed by the pedantry that had invaded even his private thoughts. This had increased since retirement, perhaps exemplifying the Goethian, or Hegelian, principle.

I cannot find my wife.

My wife is missing.

He tried out little introductory disclaimers, perhaps even a little laugh by way of preface. Nor could he decide whether to call Manfredi or Noonan. 911 was an option. That might be best. That would give the appropriate note of urgency and the person he talked to would not know who he was.

This had been on the second day. Saturday. It was possible that a little game was being played on him, Virginia joining with the others, thinking it was simply good-natured fun. They had not yet consummated their marriage, and it was impossible not to think that had something to do with Virginia's disappearance.

How he hated that word. Was Lilian laughing at him from that bourne from which no traveler returns?

As all debaters know, it is impossible to prove a negative. How could he be sure that Virginia was gone? He was almost surprised that she had left no note. Lilian at least had left a note. He read the message informing him of her leaving and everything fell into place.

On Sunday night he had returned to his old haunts in order to help old McMullin celebrate his ninetieth birthday. Once it would have seemed record setting to live to ninety, but it had become a cliché.

Every morning on television mention was made of the people who turned one hundred that day. Not an exhaustive list, just a sampling, those who had called in or, more likely, had someone call for them. Ninety seemed all the more an age everyone would reach. That had been the theme of his remarks at the McMullin party. Ambrose had mentioned a memoir by Georges Simenon, *When I Was Old*.

He had always loved parties and when Sunday rolled around he needed one. He felt absurd, not tragic. I have mislaid my wife. What Rachel could do with that remark. The parties at the Residenza had taken on a character that had been established when Lilian was still alive. It began with birthdays. The point of a birthday party was not just the meal, the cake, the getting together. Each one had to make a contribution, some doggerel of his own, or recite some work of someone else, sing a song. Among Lilian's papers would be found the contributions made, all typed out; it became a requirement that they be turned in to her for what she had called the archives. But it wasn't the record, it was the doing of what one did that mattered, the occurrence itself, the sheer fun of it all.

Alma usually sang a popular song, sometimes what she called a medley. She had a true, if thin, voice and displayed her palms as she sang, holding them up chest high. Last night it had been "Autumn Leaves." Rachel accompanied her on the piano. Rachel at the keyboard supported any performances that required it and she did it superbly well. For her own contribution she would imitate Victor Borge's manner

and technique. They all stole and borrowed shamelessly be-
cause this was just among themselves. Art imitates art. Not
everyone realized that Ambrose was borrowing a page from
Chesterton when he offered half a dozen versions of
Happy Birthday in the styles of Wallace Stevens, T. S.
Eliot, e. e. cummings, Dylan Thomas, Shakespeare and Dante.

Here I am an old man in a dry month . . .
Bartender, hurry up please, it's time—
We will serve no wine before
Or after either
We who time and time again
At the still point of the turning wheel
Hear an unoiled squeak.

On this commemoration of your nativity—
I had not thought death had undone so many . . .
Feliz navidad, happy birthday, hapless friend . . .

When read later it could be difficult to believe how de-
lightful the occasion of the first performance was. Of course,
what they were doing was showing off. There are only two
kinds of professor, hams and cured hams, and the distinction
does not lie in the fact that some are not yet retired and others
are.

It surprised people to learn that Lilian had written doggerel as dreadful as anyone's for such occasions. As Virginia
would see. Even thinking of the party was a way of not
thinking of Virginia. Friday night he had fallen asleep while
reading Hilaire Belloc whom he loved, but beloved books had
become soporifics, a pleasant way to usher in sleep. Which
was all right when one was in bed, but Friday night or early
Saturday morning he had snapped awake to find himself

seated in a chair. Belloc had tumbled to the floor. The lamp beside the chair still burned but it was the only light lit. He turned it off and listened to the alien silence of the new apartment. In the event, leaving Collier Avenue for the Residenza was less difficult than this latest move from the Residenza. There were no memories at the new address and that made it seem unfurnished indeed. Odd that Virginia had not wakened him and sent him to bed.

The door of her room was closed and he went on to his own. Five minutes later he was again asleep, this time in his pajamas and in his bed. If he had thought of it at all, he would have told himself that Virginia was in her own room; that she had gone to bed without disturbing him. But in the morning when he knocked and looked in at the made up bed and had the sudden certainty that she had not spent the night there, it seemed clear that she would have turned off the lamp beside his chair before going to her room. If she had decided not to disturb him. It was clear that she had spent the night somewhere else.

Fessing like a pro, the old professor said
he took a wife but couldn't keep
her in his castle
only God could
condescend to love her hanging hair.

2

"Your skepticism could never equal mine," Basil said to Detective Noonan who came with an aggrieved expression Basil thought he understood.

"She is missing?"

"She has not been home in three days."

"It would be four now?"

Basil smiled tolerantly. Did Noonan expect to surprise him in a lie? "Three days when I called, computing days as we do when we say that Christ rose again on the third day, that he spent three days in the tomb. She left here Friday morning, she did not return that night, nor did she return on Saturday. On Sunday I called 911."

"Did you try to find her?"

"It took time for real concern to gather, Captain."

"Manfredi is the captain, I am a mere detective."

How tempting a tangent the phrase presented, but he realized that he must avoid facetiousness at all costs. Perhaps he should have come weeping to the door. For there had been tears. On Saturday afternoon he had gone to Mass at the Newman Club, the liturgy anticipating that of Sunday. Virginia thought it marvelous that one could perform one's religious duty and still have the whole of Sunday free like all the other pagans. Basil accepted the concept; it was a matter of canon law and the Church could decide as she wished. Unlike Ambrose he had no ambition to guide the course of the Church with his theological advice. But Basil found the Newman Club's liturgy punitive. What would the great cardinal have said about the humanizing of the Mass that went on there? Father Herrick seemed costumed rather than vested, his face wore a perpetual manic smile, and he sat on the floor during his homily while the congregation sat on chairs, a dangerous angle of vision. Basil was reminded of the lecture hall with rising banked seats for students, the professor strutting and fretting his hour below, looking up at what the junior faculty had dubbed Thighland. Last Saturday the gospel reading had been the woman caught in adultery, and the homily could have been taken as a vigorous defense of marital infidelity. To take the sixth commandment literally came through as pharisaism. Not the best setting in which to wonder where one's wife had gone.

The tears? They came later that night when he was searching the house for clues and came upon the letters, bound with a rubber binder, three letters in all, that had been pushed into a pocket of Virginia's shoe holder, behind a weather-beaten pair of loafers. Hidden? When he read the return address he had no doubt of it, and his heart stood still. He stood still as well, unable to repress the remembered sound of Alma's voice. *I took one look at you, that's all I meant to do* . . . Frederick Arthur Hardie, M.D.

"Dr. Hearty?" he had said, when she first told him the name of her husband.

"You wouldn't think so if you met him."

Best not to encourage criticism of the shuffled-off spouse, but there was no need to. Virginia wanted Basil to know the story. After graduation from Loyola, FAH, as she had acronomically dubbed him in the first halcyon days of their love, was accepted at several medical schools, but chose Creighton because the cost of living in Omaha was the lowest of any of the schools. He had worked it out on the computer, finding a site that compared housing costs, food and medical costs ("I wouldn't want to practice there.") and also gave a security ranking. They went to Omaha.

"You were married before that?"

"Medical school was our honeymoon. Later . . . Oh, later, we were going to do everything. Meanwhile I worked in an insurance company office, studied and passed the required tests, and became a real estate agent. I did well."

Her story, she assured him, had the ring of banality. It happened all the time. The first wife gave way to a trophy wife once the goal of affluence was reached. Although, like her counterparts, Virginia could claim that she had financed the means of that affluence, the courts were not friendly to such pleas. Ironically, Hardie did set up his practice in Omaha. And, after the marriage crashed, Virginia resolved to attain a doctorate of her own and came to Fort Elbow.

Holding the little stack of letters, Basil faced a crisis of conscience. He had not been married to Virginia long enough to imagine that she had no secrets from him, that she had become what he and Lilian had called one another, *dimidium animae meae.* (Basil once attributed the phrase to Maritain and was gently reminded by Ambrose. "Horace, if you please.") Half my soul. ("Nor did it have any marital meaning for Horace. Or indeed female.") Ambrose sniffed. Lilian had worked out the various noises that served as punctuation for Ambrosian utterances. This sniff was the exclamation point, a plosive pop of the lips a period, inhaling through the nose the comma. The colon? Don't ask. It was when he read the letters that he cried.

Hardie's second marriage had gone bust and now, like Adolphus Crosbie in *The Last Chronicle of Barset,* he wanted to return to the woman he had loved and left. His prolonged self-pitying screeds filled Basil with contempt, and for a moment he imagined Virginia reading them with that attitude. But what woman could fail to be moved by such an abject admission of having been wrong? The first two letters were ambiguous as to what his intentions were. The second letter made it clear that Virginia had answered him. The last letter was dated a week ago and proposed that they meet and talk about it, letters were no way to discuss something so important. He would be in Chicago for a convention the following weekend. But say the word and there would be a ticket to Chicago waiting for Virginia at the Fort Elbow airport.

Basil returned the letters to their envelopes, bound them with the rubber binder and returned them to the pocket of the shoe holder from which he had taken them. He saved his tears until he was in the living room. He knew himself well enough that he felt both the pain of loss and the pleasure of lamenting it. How delicious it is to savor misfortune when it is something that was half-desired, unconsciously hoped for. Still, he wept, and wept sincerely.

But it was with something of the sense of going home that he set off for the Residenza and the McMullin birthday celebration. He would move back with his old friends and grow old along with them. It was in the course of the evening that he decided what he would do.

The first time as tragedy, the second time as farce. He telephoned 911.

3

"You're sure she left no note?"

"You can imagine how I scoured the place."

"Do you mind if I look around?"

"Not at all. In fact, I insist on it."

"Professor, after all that has happened, you can understand that I have to proceed this way."

Wonderful young man, thus providing the opportunity to be magnanimous. Basil kept with him as Noonan looked around the apartment. Did he find it as featureless as its occupant did? Nothing had an individual stamp; everything could be duplicated elsewhere. It was as if the mythical mathematical average had taken on a material existence. And yet Basil had welcomed this anonymity as the setting for his great venture with Virginia. But the great question remained unanswered. Could he or couldn't he? Had his failure to claim her, to know her in the biblical sense, made departure easier for her? How could he doubt it?

Patiently, Basil stood in the doorway of the study while Noonan rummaged around at the desk.

"This is where she worked?"

"Some, yes. Of course, there is also our office."

"We'll check that later."

Basil nodded. Is this how God feels watching his creatures act, knowing when searches were futile yet letting them go on? Thus Basil watched Noonan waste time in the study. Finally he was through.

"Where is your room?"

"Virginia had her own room."

A fleeting moment when tact was everything, and Noonan came through with blazing colors. He nodded and asked to be shown the room.

Basil sat on the bed, and again experienced the godlike knowledge that most of what Noonan was doing would yield nothing. He willed him to look into the closet. But when the detective did, he gave it hardly a glance, moved the hanging clothes as if perhaps Virginia was hiding behind them, and turned away.

"Look at the number of shoes she has."

"Did she take anything with her?"

"Let me see."

Basil went to the closet and pushed the hanging gowns to one side so that the shoe holder was in full view. Noonan stood beside him, as Basil pretended to count the dresses. How do I clothe thee, let me count the ways.

"What are those letters?" Noonan asked at last.

Basil stepped back, filled with a divine satisfaction that the earthly creature, after many efforts, finally did the right thing by accident.

"These are from her first husband?"

"So it seems."

"She hadn't told you about receiving them?"

"No."

"Of course, you would never have looked in her closet for anything."

"Virginia came to my room." He invested the statement with as much concealed meaning as he could. Noonan paused but then made the right interpretation.

"Right. In the circumstances, I think you should open these letters, Professor."

"In the circumstances, I think you should."

Noonan moved his lips only slightly when he read, frowning over the pages, stirring uncomfortably.

"I am afraid these tell the story."

"I'm ready."

Basil craved to edit the account Noonan gave of the content of the letters. He correctly inferred that the first letter had been answered, thus eliciting the second. Had the third responded to an expressed willingness by Virginia to meet with her former husband?

Noonan then used the telephone. After half an hour he had learned that no flight out of Fort Elbow had a Virginia Bauer on it.

"Try Lilian Dahl."

"Are you serious?"

"Ask them."

But Basil was spared that indignity at least. There was no Lilian Dahl on an outgoing flight on Friday, Saturday or Sunday, for that matter. There had been a medical convention in Chicago as Hardie had said.

"Was he alone?" Noonan asked the manager of the hotel when he got him on the phone.

Of course he was not given an answer to that. No Virginia Bauer or Lilian Dahl was registered at the hotel during the course of the convention.

"I don't want to telephone the doctor. It will be better if we have the Omaha police look into that."

Basil nodded. This was clearly no longer in his hands.

"Does she still own the Volvo?"

"How did you know that?"

"I first met your wife two years ago when we were investigating a suicide at the building where she lived."

"A suicide!"

"A man named Chip Bufalo."

"But how did that involve Virginia?"

"Chip Bufalo's apartment was in the same building."

"Were there only two?"

"Oh no."

This was a blow indeed. Quite obviously, Virginia had figured sufficiently in the investigation to remain in Noonan's memory. And to recall even the make of car she drove! We are all strangers to one another, but Basil found this information vertiginous.

"I didn't check the garage," he lied.

The Volvo was there, marked with all the dints and dust of years prior to his knowing Virginia, a whole unknown history parked silently there in the cool garage among the smells of oil and exhaust.

"It's there," Noonan said, when he returned.

Nothing had diminished his obvious satisfaction since reading the letters. The disappearance was solved, and the fact that Virginia's mode of leaving town was mysterious did not faze him.

"In one letter he spoke of driving her. Perhaps he came by for her on the way to Chicago."

Quite a detour, that, but the demands of theory make crooked ways straight. Noonan had his explanation, and that was that.

Basil feared that he was right.

"Tell me about the man who committed suicide."

Manfredi

1

Noonan—this was the gist of Noonan's report—had cracked the case first shot out of the box.

"The letters were a surprise to him?"

"They were squirreled away in her closet. They have separate bedrooms." Noonan paused. Let silence be eloquent. "She had stuffed them away in a gizmo that holds shoes in pockets."

"Funny she left them," Manfredi said.

"I told Professor Bauer we would return them."

Professor Bauer. "Does he want them?"

"He wants his wife."

Had a wife and couldn't keep her. Had two, in Basil's case, making him twice as vulnerable to taunting as Peter Peter Pumpkin Eater.

"These letters suggest she has gone off to see her first husband."

"Only we don't know how she went off," Noonan said. "I checked the airport. She didn't fly out of here. I checked the hotel in Chicago. She wasn't registered there. Funny thing."

"What?"

"Basil told me to try under Lilian Dahl as well as Virginia Bauer."

"How about Virginia Hardie?"

Noonan's mouth formed an O.

"What was her maiden name? Check that out too."

150

And then, because this seemed to be taking some of the wind out of Noonan's sails, he added, "Good work."

"Yeah."

A moment later, Gloria came in and blew him a kiss. Credit and blame are seldom closely linked to what one actually does or does not do. Quote me. Manfredi was addressing the mental monitor whose volume he had recently increased. He was acting under the surveillance of his most demanding professional conscience. Gloria's tribute, however misdirected, was nonetheless welcome. His monitor was giving him far lower grades.

But how could he be blamed, even though it was undeniably true that his interviews with Alma and Rachel and Ambrose would have been more productive if he had known about those letters from her former husband. Separate bedrooms. What did it matter? There could not be much mattress acrobatics involved in that odd May and December marriage. For the imagined pleasure of Alma, he mentally did a superb silent imitation of Ezio Pinza. "Once you have found her, never let her go." Poor Basil. How could he compete with the chance to forgive the rat who had thrown her aside like a used Kleenex? That might be more fulfilling than pretending you were a dead poet.

Noonan came back in half an hour, having drawn blanks in every try.

"If she had a way to get to Cleveland she could have flown from there," Manfredi suggested.

"I thought of that."

"No luck?"

"Of course she could have been using a fourth name."

"And hitchhiked to Cleveland."

"Why not to Chicago?"

"Why not indeed?"

One impossibility entailed others in the sense that it failed to exclude it.

"That could still be what happened. Have you gotten in touch with the Omaha police?"

He had. They would discreetly find out if Dr. Hardie had been rejoined by his first wife.

"They liked the description of her."

"The name of the race track down there is Aksarben."

"I don't gamble."

"That's Nebraska spelled backward."

"How did you know that?"

"I gamble."

2

It seemed fitting that she should have three names. Manfredi found it difficult to put together the woman who had worked to put her husband through medical school, the occupant of the apartment building who had swapped keys with an eventual suicide, and the darling of the Fort Elbow emeriti whose lives had been inextricably linked with Lilian Dahl. And now she was the wife, albeit missing, of Basil Bauer, who had been married in a previous mythical time to the gifted poet.

Why would she marry Basil and then go off with her former husband? The first letter was dated before the wedding. There was a three-week lapse until the next letter, it too written prior to the wedding. The third had arrived a week ago when she was definitively Mrs. Basil Bauer. The envelopes were addressed to Virginia Hardie, care of the Department of English at Fort Elbow. Divorcees retain their married names, of course, but it was not as Virginia Hardie that she had been known in Fort Elbow. Manfredi telephoned the registrar at the university.

"I want to make an inquiry about a graduate student."

"For what purpose?"

"This is Egidio Manfredi, captain of detectives, Fort Elbow police."

"I cannot verify that on the telephone."

"Hear me out. We have received a missing person report on a woman who, among other things, is a graduate student in English at the university."

"She is missing?"

"That is her husband's claim. Now, I can come out there and show you my badge. I can come with a court order to examine your records. That will take time. My disposition will be affected if we go that route, and so will yours. Meanwhile, the safety of a young woman may be in question. Are you with me?"

"Go ahead."

"She receives her mail at the departmental office as Virginia Hardie."

"What department?"

"English."

"Just a moment."

The click and purr of a computer became audible. Bursts of clicking keys, a pause, another burst, a world of data at the fingertips.

"There is a person of that name registered as a graduate student in English. What do you want to know?"

Manfredi had already found out the main thing, she had indeed used her married name as a student. But she had rented her apartment as Virginia Wilson, and that is how Basil and the others had known her. If she had used the name Virginia Hardie at the apartment, would Noonan have made the connection, or simply dismissed it as a case of look-alikes?

153

The address and phone number the registrar had were not those of her cohabitation with Basil. Nothing significant in that, to be sure. There might not have been an occasion yet to make the correction.

"You said you were a captain."

"Captain of detectives. Manfredi."

"There is a note in her folder indicating another inquiry was made about her. A Doctor Hardie in Omaha. Since he was a relative, he was given her campus address."

"Dr. Frederick Arthur Hardie?"

"Oh good, you know him."

"How long ago did he make that inquiry?"

Two months ago, prior to the first letter.

3

"She was practically a child bride, I understand." Alma settled her dress about her as she sat.

"She had reached the age of consent."

"What a poignant phrase."

"She was nineteen."

"Why am I shocked? I was not yet twenty-one when I married. It shocks me to think of that. What did I think I was doing? All my children were older than I had been when I married, older by several years, twelve in one case, and they still didn't seem old enough to look after themselves."

Alma had known of Virginia's first marriage, but she had placed it in the very remote past. But if Virginia had been young when she married, the marriage itself had lasted almost a decade.

"He has written to her lately. His second marriage failed, now he wants to go back to square one."

"That's just where she would be if she took him. Just a

good-hearted woman in love with a two-timing man."

"Country western?"

"Un-huh. So that's what this comes down to, the bride debouches to her first spouse?"

"That's the tempting explanation. It would give a motive, it would give a destination, maybe it would explain why she left without explaining it to Basil."

"Poor Basil. How ridiculous to think he could bring back the golden years with Lilian by marrying again."

"You think that's what it was?"

"The girl is obviously a surrogate. Basil doubtless imagines that he is passionately in love with her, age not taking on him the toll it takes on the rest of us."

"You're a fine one to talk."

Alma burst into song. "You picked a fine time to leave me, Lucille."

"That's pretty."

"Kenny Rogers."

"How would Virginia leave town if she didn't drive and she didn't fly."

"Train?"

Manfredi looked at her. The Fort Elbow station had been converted into a kind of mall, with restaurants, shops, a banquet hall.

"Amtrak comes through Ann Arbor on its way to Chicago."

"But how would she have gotten to Ann Arbor?"

Alma told him of the bulletin boards on campus, festooned with notes offering or seeking rides to various places.

"Usually these are on the weekend, kids going home."

"And I had discounted hitchhiking."

"Oh, this is far more socially acceptable than hitchhiking."

★ ★ ★ ★ ★

He and Noonan went to the campus together and went from bulletin board to bulletin board, those in the dorms and classroom building featuring, among other things, bids and offers of rides. There were several Detroits and one Grand Rapids, but no Ann Arbor.

"She might have removed it when she found it so no one else could call before she did."

They were reduced finally to visiting the registrar and meeting Richard in the flesh, about two hundred and fifty pounds of flesh. He turned away and held up his hand to shield his eyes when they displayed their badges.

"I had to ask those questions."

"If you hadn't we would have arrested you."

"Honestly?"

"Divulging confidential information is a federal crime."

"What I told you, you could have learned from calling the English Department."

"We have another request."

"If I can legally cooperate," Richard said in wounded tones.

"We want the names of all the students who come from Ann Arbor."

"Is that all?"

But he wasn't being ironic. The search program that had been designed for the registrar's office permitted far more demanding searches than this one. There were seventeen students from Ann Arbor. Richard printed out the list for them, including their campus and home numbers.

"With the names and the campus phone book, you could find these out yourself."

"Ever thought of becoming a cop?"

"I could never make the weight."

"We have a new heavyweight division."

Richard pursed his lips and wrinkled his nose. "Get out of here."

4

Routine is a wonderful thing. The mechanization of information is a wonderful thing. The telephone, fax and e-mail deserved and got Manfredi's applause. But put them all together and they gave the following results.

Of the seventeen Ann Arbor residents attending the Fort Elbow campus, two had been home during the past weekend and both had driven.

Of the two, one, Larry Broderick took a passenger, gave another student a lift, the ride arranged via a bulletin board notice. Was the passenger male or female? Female. Her name? He didn't remember. All he would have remembered was the first name, but he wasn't sure of that. How often do you use another's name in conversation with them? Besides, it was simply an arrangement of convenience, she paid for the gas, which was no big deal. The distance from Fort Elbow to Ann Arbor not being great.

Where had Broderick dropped off his passenger? At the Amtrak station. Manfredi gave a description of Virginia, getting approving nods from Noonan as he did. Everything jibed.

"Why do you say old though? This girl was young. I think she said she was a freshman."

This brought all the cards that had gone into the construction of the house crashing down.

Were they at a point where they could rule out the Hardie letters as explanatory of Virginia's absence? There were unrecorded ways of getting out of Fort Elbow, and if she had indeed gone to Ann Arbor, train tickets were not sold in the name of the purchaser. Amtrak was an anonymous way to travel.

And there was the bus. The Fort Elbow bus station had become an unsavory place in recent years, with derelicts and other furtive types haunting the premises. The men's room was a constant source of police business. But one did not have to take up residence in the depot in order to board a bus. She could have taken a bus without it being recorded.

"And there is the Airport Limo," Noonan suddenly remembered. This was a rather grandly-named bus that took people to the Detroit and Cleveland airports from Fort Elbow, a blessing to those travelers for whom the hang gliders the feeder lines flew in and out of Fort Elbow were too terrifying to contemplate.

"That takes us back to the airline records, however."

"So we have learned nothing."

Not quite. They knew what they did not know. And what they did not know did not exclude and could continue to include what had actually happened. She could have gotten a ride to the Amtrak in Ann Arbor and gone on to Chicago without any record being made of it. She could have gone by bus.

"But she wasn't registered at the hotel."

"In any name we know. I suppose it is unrealistic to suppose that she would share a room with Hardie."

"Maybe she really is missing," Noonan said.

"That can't be ruled out."

Rachel

1

Basil confided in Rachel about the letters from her first husband that Virginia had hidden in her closet.

"Remember this is an old friend speaking, Basil, and I say good riddance."

"Rachel!"

"Think about it. Hiding letters at the beginning of a marriage. What kind of start is that?"

"It isn't her fault he wrote to her."

"But she kept them. She must have answered, else why more letters?"

"I suppose you're right." Basil groaned. "Rachel, I have no allusions as to how attractive to a young woman marriage to a man in his seventies can be. I'll tell you a secret. I thought it was her interest in Lilian's papers that would keep us together until death do us part. I still cannot believe that she just walked away from that treasure."

"Another proof of how little you knew her. Why should those papers mean the same to her as they do to us?"

"Lilian's reputation as a poet is not confined to us, Rachel. She is anthologized everywhere. Just keeping track of permissions and new printings is a chore. A labor of love, but a chore. I had counted on Virginia to be of help to me there as well."

"Have you checked the papers since she left?"

"They are at the office now, most of them."

"Are you sure?"

"Of course I'm sure. It was no small thing to transfer them down there from the Residenza."

"Basil, I mean are they still *there?* Maybe she left you and not the papers. The papers she could have taken with her."

"Talking with you is always such a consolation."

"You have to check. I'll drive you down."

"Rachel, do you have any idea how many papers there are?"

"How did you get them down there?"

"We loaded both our cars. It would take a small truck to hold them all."

"Of the kind they rent?"

Rachel did not expect abject capitulation or even the admission that what she suggested was plausible. Mere possibility would do and Basil's expression made it clear that he was imagining a small truck pulling up to the office in the mall and carting off Lilian's papers. Basil went to his desk and pulled open the central drawer. He took something from it and picked up the phone.

"Basil Bauer, Mr. Knutson. You may remember that I am renting an office . . ."

Basil glanced at Rachel as he listened. "No, it wasn't I. What kind of damage is there?" Basil avoided Rachel's eyes now. "I'd have to check. Yes, of course the police should be notified. You might ask for Captain Manfredi."

"What was that all about?" Rachel asked when Basil hung up.

"Knutson thinks someone broke into the office."

"Didn't Virginia have a key?"

Basil professed to be astonished that she should link Virginia and the break-in at the office, but of course that was mere pretense. Why hadn't he checked at the office anyway?

"Basil, if I were you I would be the one who got in touch with Manfredi about this."

"Rachel, if you were me you would be a nervous wreck."

"I can manage that without being you."

"Why didn't you and I fall in love? We could have argued all the time."

"Why didn't we? Basil, I have been throwing myself at your feet ever since you became a widower. You could have had maturity, brains and a body too, and—well, it's too late now."

"Is it, Rachel?"

The dog. Rachel instinctively dismissed all overtures as attempts at humor.

"Being the wife of Basil Bauer is not a long-term occupation."

"Rachel."

"Call Manfredi."

2

To the superficial feminine eye Basil needed only direct commands in order to be brought to his own ultimate end which happily coincided with the female commandant's. That this was not true could be learned on the basis of experience, or be rationally concluded from the fact that Basil had spent the majority of his adult life without any female in a position to issue him direct commands. Rachel, having arrived at this truth by both paths, proceeded accordingly.

"Call Manfredi."

"Let Knutson do that."

"And have Manfredi relay the news to you?"

"Perhaps I will call him."

"Do it."

Basil procrastinated. However effective, obliquity is taxing. Eventually, Rachel drove Basil to his office near the mall. They were there waiting when Manfredi, summoned by Knutson, arrived.

"You haven't heard from your wife?"

"No," Basil bleated. "Have you?"

"I am simply establishing that she is still a missing person."

Knutson's short arms stood out from his body and he walked with a rolling gait. His greying crewcut drew attention to his ears, which moved in expressive accompaniment when he spoke or listened. He addressed all men as sir and called Rachel darling. Rachel could just hear Alma break into song.

You call everybody darling,
and everybody calls you darling too,
you don't mean what you're saying,
It's just a game you're playing,
but I can play that game as well as you.

"You're the one who noticed there had been a break-in?"

"No sir."

"Who did?"

"Security personnel. They reported to me what looked to be damage to the door. Apparently it had been jimmied."

"Apparently."

"Yes sir."

"I meant why apparently?"

"Because that would have set off the alarm."

"So why was the door apparently jimmied?"

"Just a guess, sir, but to make it look as if forcible entry had been made."

Basil nodded when Manfredi suggested that they go inside. The switch bathed the offices in a light that seemed to come from everywhere and nowhere. It was a marvel of smooth modernity, off white walls, soft grey cabinets.

"This is what caught Jenny's attention."

"Jenny?"

"Security."

"She been in here?"

"He sir, Jensen. No sir. He called me and I called Mr. Bauer who instructed me to call you."

What had caught Jensen's eye were the drawers of a file cabinet that had been pulled open and left open.

"What was in those cabinets?"

Basil looked puzzled. "I wish Virginia was here."

"Maybe she was."

Basil's mouth opened and, like the file cabinet drawers, stayed open. He was the last person there who made the connection between the rifling of the office and the missing Virginia.

Basil flipped through the file cabinet drawers like an indecisive bridge player. He was asked to notice if anything else had been disturbed. Meanwhile Rachel roamed around the office that Virginia had furnished and arranged. Basil's room had all the trappings of authority but her own work area, as Rachel was sure she called it, was clearly the heart of the enterprise. When Basil was here he could sit in his own room, revolve in his executive chair and look through the slanted blinds of his windows at the getting and spending going on at the mall. Rachel saw no evidence of any work having been done in the office. Basil was now examining a cabinet filled with archival boxes, a darker grey than the cabinet. She flicked on the computer in Basil's office and ran a directory. Stored on it were the files of Basil's interminable book and little else. Had the book advanced since his liaison with Virginia? All these files bore the same date, when they would have been transferred to this computer, shortly after they had taken possession of this office.

Had Basil needed the illusion that he was still at work, that there was this office to which he came daily to fulfill a number of crucial tasks? Rachel doubted it. The leisurely pace of the Residenza was more commensurate with his years, more contemplative.

Basil said that he was certain something was missing.

Manfredi told him to take his time. How I love that man, Rachel thought, then asked herself which one. Both, came the reply, but for different reasons. The remark had been prompted by the droll irony of Manfredi's voice, but Basil's baffled quest for what might be missing from the papers, what his second wife had stolen of his first wife's papers, that is, further endeared him to her.

Rachel made coffee in the little kitchenette after Manfredi had checked the room to see if anything was obviously amiss. The smell of coffee swiftly filled the suite of rooms.

"There's tea there too, Rachel."

Tea for two and two for tea, a boy for you a girl for me. Was that right? Manfredi's assistant, Detective Noonan, arrived. How eagerly he listened as Manfredi brought him up to date. Knutson was brought into it and sirred them both right and left.

"Well look who's here," Noonan exclaimed when he noticed Rachel.

"They caught me working on the safe. I want to call my lawyer."

But a eureka went up from Basil. He sat back in his chair,

his arms hanging down, an expression of self-deprecating understanding on his face.

"It's so obvious that of course I missed it."

"What?"

"Lilian's notebooks!" They had marched along two shelves of a cabinet and marched no more. They were all missing.

"They are of course invaluable, biographically, but why those rather than other things?"

"Isn't Virginia writing a life of Lilian?" Rachel asked.

"Of course."

3

Basil was weary and preoccupied on the drive back to the Residenza. He leaned back against the headrest and closed his eyes.

"I will never forgive you for that cock and bull story about killing Lilian and throwing her body into the river."

"You owe me undying gratitude for that."

"You're going to tell me why."

"I am. What if there had been only Ambrose's story of what had happened?"

"Why did he come up with such nonsense?"

"Oh his story was probably true."

"Rachel!"

Manfredi

1

Marian Casey had been made unhappy by the publicity given Ambrose Hennessy's claim that he had killed Lilian Dahl and buried her body in the greenhouse of her former home. That was the house on Collier Street that Marian Casey had on the market for a huge sum. After Ambrose's story, the fact that the house on Collier had once been the home of the famous poet Lilian Dahl was not the plus it had been.

"Should I tell them she's buried on the premises?" she asked Manfredi.

"What do you want me to do?"

"Tear up the floor and find out one way or another."

"Hennessy was just talking. Do you want me to have the river dragged because Rachel Salma said she killed Lilian and threw the body in the river?"

"What's wrong with those people?"

"It's called the life of the mind."

"I would dig up the floor myself but for two things. One, I don't want to run into anything grisly, and, two, if I did find her body I would get publicity of the same kind the story got. But not if I didn't."

"Marian, the only reason I would get a court order to look under that greenhouse floor would be if I believed Ambrose Hennessy's story."

"Would you buy the house under these circumstances?"

"I have a house."

"Don't tell me you want to sell it."

Manfredi had several times asked Marian what she thought he could get for his house. He and Teresa no longer needed so large a place, that was the idea, although whenever they looked at smaller places they couldn't imagine living there.

"We'd be bumping into one another all the time."

Meaning they were used to the buffer of more rooms than they needed. Manfredi now found it hard to believe they had all once fitted into that house.

"Why did Basil Bauer move out of the house on Collier Avenue? His friends could have moved in with him. There would have been plenty of room, they would have saved money and they could have hired a housekeeper."

"You should ask him."

"What's the point now? I have nearly sold that house on Collier to myself several times."

"Really." He gave her a lidded look. It sounded like part of a sale's pitch.

"I just love that house. Can't you see yourself, out on that veranda on a summer evening, under all those marvelous trees? The plot is two acres, you know."

"Two acres?"

"There was some objection against dividing it to conform to the usual size of city lots."

"Objection from whom?"

"Of course all this land originally belonged to the Indians. Every plat book takes the lot in question back to Andrew Jackson's presidency."

"What was their objection?"

Marian smiled in a way that expressed more pain than joy. "They said it was a burial ground."

How could she be otherwise than serious about this?

167

Manfredi forbore expressing the hilarity he felt.

"There's your solution, Marian. Refer to the place as built on the traditional burial grounds of native Americans. You can turn it into a plus."

"I knew I shouldn't have told you."

"I'll bet Ambrose Hennessy knew this. He was trying to snooker me into desecrating the burial grounds of native Americans."

"Who would think that if you simply looked under the floor of the greenhouse?"

"You have seen what publicity can do."

"I suppose I'll just have to ride it out. Meanwhile, that lovely house stands empty."

"You could ask Hennessy to recant publicly."

"That would only make things worse. Then people would have to forget it all over again."

"I guess you'll have to buy it yourself."

"I'm almost afraid to."

"You could make it a shrine. A tourist attraction."

"Is Lilian Dahl really that important a poet?"

"I was thinking of the Indian burial grounds."

2

"Let's go out there."

"Oh good."

"I'm not bringing a shovel, Marian. I just want to see the place."

"It would be perfect for you and Teresa."

"We could call it Requiem House."

"You're awful."

Collier Avenue antedated the platting of the city of Fort Elbow, being originally the trail on which settlers moved from Ohio on into Michigan and Indiana before those states were states. When the platting was done, Collier ran diagonally across the geometry of the city and the lots along it were appreciably larger than elsewhere, since they were not subject to the same linear restraints. The lots grew larger as one went west and, in the case of the lot on which Basil Bauer's former house stood, because of the additional reason of the real or alleged burial grounds, was a full two acres.

Collier was a pleasant street to come along, perhaps one of the most gracious in Fort Elbow. The houses stood well back on their lots and had been built with the confidence of those whom life has treated well. The erstwhile Basil Bauer house, as has been mentioned, was said to be in the prairie style, but there seemed no evidence of direct influence. The architect had been a local engineer, Chris Policinski, for whom architecture was almost a hobby. He had designed four houses in the city, two of which were still standing.

A driveway twisted under the trees and came to the double garages which, though a later addition, were attached to the house. The house itself was brick and had in effect two main entrances. One to which stairs from the driveway led and another on the side facing the street, which was reached by a veranda embracing two sides of the house in a great right angle. The eaves of both the porch and of the roof extended out beyond the usual distances and it was this, along with the sense of arranged planes that gave rise to the likening of the house to those of Frank Lloyd Wright. The greenhouse was not immediately visible when they parked in the driveway. It sloped off from the west end of the garage, on the far side from the house, its glass angling down from just below roof level. A large shrub in need of trimming made the greenhouse all but invisible.

"Why don't we go through the house?"

"Don't you have a key to the garage?"

"But you have to see this place."

Why not? This after all was the house in which Lilian Dahl had dwelt. Marian had asked if she were as great a poet as all that, and of course Manfredi was no judge, but a quick check had shown that she was included in most standard anthologies of American poetry, which seemed fame enough. And Virginia had not been the first one to think of writing her biography.

Her proposed dissertation on the work of the poet had led Virginia from the poetry itself to the poet and that in turn had led to her acquaintance with Basil Bauer who became in effect her patron. At his suggestion and with his blessing she had submitted a proposal for a biography of Lilian Dahl to the poet's publisher and it had been accepted enthusiastically.

"The authorized biography," Alma had explained to Manfredi.

"As opposed to what?"

"As opposed to two others that had been either announced or contracted for, under somewhat false pretensions."

"Hmmm."

"Shall I go on?"

Manfredi could have listened to Alma read the telephone directory. He nodded.

And thus it was that he got Alma's version of the two authors, Felicia Christman and Ben Ventuti, whose careers had been destroyed by Basil's anointing of Virginia as the official biographer of his late wife.

"And she always was."

"What?"

"Late. Make an appointment and add a half hour at least

before she would actually show up."

"You were telling me about disgruntled authors."

"Why do I get the feeling that you are humoring me?"

"I took one look at you, that's all I meant to do . . ."

Alma could not resist taking up the tune and her sassy little voice added to the pleasure of Manfredi's afternoon. But she did get back to Christman and Ventuti and their thwarted careers.

"Ventuti threatened her bodily. I think Felicia Christman made a Virginia doll to stick pins into. Of course she had lied to her publisher that she had been dubbed Lilian's biographer by Basil. Ventuti had done something similarly unprofessional."

"So they dropped the idea entirely."

"Sweetheart, without those papers, a life of Lilian would be little more than critical marginalia on the poems. Such books will be written; several have already appeared, but no one would mistake them for a biography. Virginia had acquired access to the papers and that was the trump. Marrying Basil sealed the bargain."

"No wonder she ran away."

"Don't you believe it."

Now, in the house where the poet had lived, the house from which one day she had fled, Manfredi allowed himself to feel her presence.

"It's not my sort of thing," Teresa had said, when he asked her to read Lilian's poems.

Well, no one thought of her as a ladies' poet, feminine as her imagination had been. She had been likened to Edna St. Vincent Millay in her appeal to male readers.

"Lilian Dahl wrote several poems about this house."

"How do you know these things?"

"I'm a detective."

171

My house of flesh and bone
is houseled here in stone
and brick;
the wick
of life will not outlast
this house that casts
its shadow
on that living lawn
and will when I am gone
for years and years
until it also disappears.

"Nice," Marian said.

"You're patronizing me."

"But sad. I'm trying to sell the house."

The front entrance opened into a vestibule that then gave way to a large hall from which a magnificent stairway rose to huge windows on the landing. The living room was to the left of the hall, through French doors, a room that ran the whole width of the house with the fireplace at one end flanked by built-in bookshelves. On the other side of the hall were the kitchen and dining room, each accessible from the hall. Joined by another door and at the back of the house, as much windows as shelves, was the study that looked out on what had been a grove of fruit trees retained now but for their beauty.

Marian insisted that he see the upstairs as well. Again a huge hall, a room in itself, with four bedrooms opening off it.

"But only one bath," Marian whispered.

The proliferation of bathrooms, half baths, basement showers, in recent housing made this stately house with but one large bathroom upstairs seem odd indeed.

"Uncanny."

Marian made a face. "But then one bathed on Saturday."

"Monday washday."

"Tuesday ironing. Is that right?"

"I have no idea."

And so downstairs and through the kitchen into the back hall and the entrance to the garage. Manfredi had expected the garage to be illumined by the greenhouse, but Marian had to flip a switch before they could proceed. The door that gave admittance to the greenhouse had a small window, not enough to dispel the darkness of the garage. The door was locked from within, a sliding bolt. When Marian opened the door there came a rush of hot, stale, sweet and sour, fetid air. She stepped aside to make way for Manfredi, but he stood in the doorway and did not descend the little stairway to the floor level of the greenhouse, already four or five feet below ground level.

"Getting down to six feet would be easy."

Marian waved away his explanation before he gave it.

There were vases hanging from various hooks, their contents shriveled and dead. Pan-like shelves hung at various levels, filled with terra cotta pots, some of which contained dirt as dry as dust. The greenhouse had become a cemetery of vegetative life. There was a solid u-shaped workbench at the level at which the squared panes of glass began and on it the trappings of the gardener. On one arm of this working surface, dusty boxes filled with fertilizer, aids to growth, and other promissory notes, made an irregular row.

"The floor even looks temporary."

The bricks were laid unmortared in a pattern of chevrons. Manfredi went down to floor level, knelt and pried loose a brick.

"Take them all up," Marian urged.

He replaced the brick and stood. *Requiescat in pace.*

173

Marian made an impatient noise. But when Manfredi looked up she was furtively blessing herself.

3

With the negative news from Omaha—there had been no reunion of the Hardies—and the inconclusiveness, to put the best face on it, of the inquiry into how Virginia might have left Fort Elbow, Basil told Manfredi that he had given up hope.

"Captain, I fear the worst."

"Professor, it makes no sense, her leaving. She was writing the life of your wife."

"But all the notebooks are gone. They are the richest source of information. The letters, too, of course . . ."

"Could the notebooks be here?"

They were speaking in the apartment Virginia and Basil had rented when he moved out of the Residenza.

"Perhaps in her closet?" he said wryly.

They were not in her closet. They were nowhere in the apartment.

"Captain, it occurs to me that it would not even count as theft. She is my wife . . ."

"If we can find her, I don't think we will worry about what she may have taken."

"May have taken. You are right. It is after all an assumption. Someone tried to break into the office."

"Well, someone tried to make it look like a break-in, but the door had been opened with a key, otherwise the alarm would have gone off. And who had a key besides Virginia and Basil?"

"Knutson."

"And no one else?"

Basil shook his head but his thoughtful expression suggested that his mind had traveled on. He became grave.

"Captain, I have the strongest suspicion that Ambrose Hennessy is behind this."

"Your friend?"

"The friend of my youth, of my maturity, of my old age. Yes. Don't forget his confession. He counted on not being taken seriously, but it would be like Ambrose to make a clean breast of things while keeping his shirt on."

"It was to killing Lilian that he confessed."

"But that was an expression of resentment."

"Of what?"

"Of whom. Me. Captain, we have been rivals since we were thirteen. I know Ambrose better than I know myself, and vice versa. Let me tell you a story that will help you understand his character."

Nearly sixty years before, in the refectory of Dowling Hall, after the other students had left, Ambrose and Basil and two other boys, the Corbett twins, were having a belated meal because it was their week to serve as student waiters. Ambrose had ascended to the pulpit which was built into a side wall of the refectory. From it the martyrology was read each noon and, before the evening meal, something from the New Testament. The boys listened with bowed heads while from the raised faculty table, half a dozen priests looked out over their charges. During the annual retreat, when silence was observed, something edifying was read throughout the meal.

"Fiends, no ones and city-dwellers," Ambrose began and in a moment had everyone's attention. He went on, improvising a variation on Marc Antony's speech. Suddenly a baked potato sailed toward the pulpit. Within a minute, a barrage of food was directed at Ambrose. He picked up what he could and hurled it back, descending from the pulpit and retreating to the kitchen, giving as good as he got as he went.

And then he disappeared behind the swinging doors just as the rector entered and saw four boys pelting the kitchen doors with food.

Silence fell. In the presence of Father Thomas, the utter stupidity of what they were doing was blindingly clear. His expression was almost punishment enough. Not to be thought well of by Father Thomas was catastrophic, not because he was cruel, but because he was kind. Finally he spoke.

"I will see all of you in my office as soon as you have cleaned up this mess."

When Father Thomas had gone, Ambrose emerged from the kitchen. He seemed prelapsarian in his innocence, having been out of range of Father Thomas's reproachful gaze.

"We have to report to his office as soon as we clean up."

Ambrose helped clean up but when that was done and one of the Corbetts said, "Let's go," it became clear that Ambrose did not consider himself one of the guilty party.

"But you were throwing food too!"

"In self-defense. You started it."

"Ambrose, he meant whoever made this mess."

Basil had sat back in his chair as if he could see that long ago scene replayed before his eyes.

"Did he go to the rector with you?" Manfredi asked.

"No."

"What was your punishment?"

"We had to stay on for an extra day when the others left for Christmas vacation. Father Thomas left it up to us what we would tell our parents."

"And Ambrose left with the others?"

"He did. But before vacation came there was a whole month in which he agonized over what he was doing. He became the hero of a moral drama that made him so much more interesting than the rest of us. He demanded that we see how difficult it was for him. We had been caught red-handed by the rector; he would have to accuse himself. He succeeded in making us all think that there was nothing quite like the difficulty he was in. He made confessing seem the easier course to bearing his load of ambiguous guilt. In the end he went home with the others."

"Interesting."

"Interesting! It is foundational. Ambrose wants the luxury of guilt without the consequence of punishment."

"As when he confessed to killing Lilian."

Basil nodded. "Ambrose is no fool. He convinced others but not himself. I came to realize that he envied those of us who were caught and punished. Envied and resented us. He wrote a comic play at the end of the year which was performed with great success. It located the food fight in a monastery and it is four novices who are caught having a food fight. The four were presented as buffoons. This was Ambrose's revenge on our unearned moral superiority. Do you know what was most difficult? During the performance I turned and saw how the faculty was enjoying it. Father Thomas was laughing heartily."

"So Ambrose is jealous of you?"

"Oh, it is mutual. We are jealous of one another. When Lilian and I fell in love, Ambrose inevitably tried to seduce her. She told me all about it."

"Yet you remained friends."

"There are no enemies like old friends."

Manfredi listened with fascination, but was unable to see the seventy-two-year-old Ambrose as one who would do harm to Virginia. More likely it would be someone like Felicia Christman or Ben Ventuti.

If indeed any harm had come to her.

4

Gregory, Basil's financial wizard son, had not come for the wedding, but he flew out to Fort Elbow now when his father was going through an experience not unlike that he had gone through with Gregory's mother.

"What progress have you made?" He sat on the opposite side of Manfredi's desk, a confident and successful young man, demanding an accounting of the investigation into his father's missing wife.

In telling Gregory Bauer what they had learned so far, Manfredi was painfully aware that he was recounting one failed effort after another. It did not help that Gregory sat without expression through the recital. And he remained silent after Manfredi had finished. When he spoke it was harshly.

"That is the biggest bunch of crap I've ever heard. You haven't a clue what happened to her, do you? It sounds to me like you have a running seminar with my father going, dreaming of unlikely explanations."

"We are simply following routine."

"Then you ought to change the routine. This is the second time this has happened to my family, Captain. When I was a kid my mother disappeared and she might have been assumed into heaven for all the police were able to find out."

"The missing notebooks . . ."

"Forget those goddamn papers. This woman is not likely to run away, and not because she couldn't bear to be separated from my mother's papers. Do you know what she came into when she married my father? He may strike you as an impractical old gent, that's what I thought myself. But the last time I was home we discussed his financial situation. I wanted to learn how long he could afford the kind of life he had at the Residenza. My father turns out to be worth something like ten million dollars."

"Ten million!"

"How could a professor whose maximum salary was less than sixty thousand a year and who began teaching for the magnificent salary of four thousand dollars, accumulate that kind of money? By getting into the market in a small way when he could hardly afford it. He has held some blue chips for forty years. I don't have to tell you what they're worth now. They have split and split again, he has continued to add modestly to his portfolio, the market value of which is nine million dollars."

"You said ten."

"His retirement account is worth another million. That too has been accumulated over four decades. My father is an old man. Would a young wife who will inherit that kind of money hop on a bus with an armful of notebooks and disappear?"

"Does she know about the money?"

"My father laid it all out for her. He showed her the report I did for him."

"That's what you do for a living, financial consultant?"

"My father's case makes me feel superfluous. He asked me to take charge of his portfolio, and I made him promise he would never let me or anyone else give him any advice whatsoever. His method is unbeatable. Buy and hang on to what you buy. He doesn't even read the financial page."

What Gregory had said certainly put a different light on things. The young man was insistent on what it illumined.

"She didn't run away. I doubt if she is still alive."

"Money can hardly provide a motive for someone else to harm her."

"No, but it proves that she did not take a walk. There is another motive for harming her."

Manfredi remained silent after Gregory had spoken. As his father's son, he had a right to come in and question the effectiveness of the police investigation. He could not be more annoyed by the lack of results than Manfredi. But there was no point in trying to justify himself to Gregory. Excluding certain possibilities is a gain in an investigation, but they do not amount to an explanation of what happened.

"You want a suggestion?"

Manfredi opened his palms receptively.

"Tear up the floor of the greenhouse at the old house."

5

Shannon the coroner looked up at Manfredi with widened eyes. He nodded.

"I'll put young Sanguinetti on it with you, but it sounds to me as though you need an archeologist not a coroner."

"What is a body like after thirty years?"

"It isn't. Hope for bones at best."

Shannon's mouth was greasy from the Big Mac he was eating and his hands were dripping with catsup. He took another large bite.

"I hope it doesn't get around that the coroner is eating at work."

Manfredi had the court order that covered an unusual search of private property. Judge Derecho had obviously studied the matter carefully.

"Has this been okayed with our native American friends, Captain?"

"Yes, your honor."

"Is there any documentation to that effect?"

"The representatives of the local tribe say they have become more than skeptical of the treatment they have received. Chief Ronald Campeau and an assistant will be there when we take up the floor of the greenhouse. The fact is they have only vague information about the whereabouts of the burial ground."

Derecho, in any case, was satisfied that sensibilities were being given consideration.

Marian Casey, needless to say, was ecstatic. She had arranged for maximum media coverage of the event, print and television. She was a little doubtful of the benefit of having the Native Americans present or any reference to burial grounds.

"Still, if he can lay the ghost of the corpse under the greenhouse floor, I will be happy."

Gregory Bauer would be there representing his father. Ambrose Hennessy had invited himself but kept sheepishly in the background. With Noonan and himself, Campeau and his aide, young Sanguinetti, who turned out to be a stunning brunette, Marian and all the media, there was the promise of a circus. Noonan hit upon the solution of lining people up on the outside of the greenhouse. Since it was all windows, they had a better view from there than if they had crowded into the garage and tried to look over shoulders to see what was going on through the narrow doorway to the greenhouse. Manfredi, Sanguinetti and Campeau went through the garage and into the greenhouse. The others were all out there, staring in at them. Gregory Bauer was obviously taken by Sarah Sanguinetti and the young pathologist had an eye on the financier as well.

"Can you hear me?" Manfredi called out.

"Open those side windows wider."

Manfredi did this. "I am Captain Egidio Manfredi, this is

Dr. Sarah Sanguinetti of the coroner's office. To her right is Chief Ronald Campeau of the Miami nation. In response to a number of claims and rumors, I am going to take up the floor of the greenhouse. It consists of loose bricks in sand. Then I am going to dig." Manfredi displayed a spade. "You will all be witnesses of the results, if any."

Campeau was at first reluctant to lend a hand, but when Dr. Sanguinetti began to stack the bricks Manfredi removed, the chief decided it was not beneath his dignity to cooperate. In a few minutes, the brick floor had become sand. Manfredi took up the shovel.

"Hold it there, Captain."

A video camera was thrust through one of the open windows and whirred, getting a good shot of the floor. Then Manfredi began digging. His plan was to transfer the dirt dug up from beneath the working surface of the greenhouse into bushel baskets. But when he had put two scoops into a basket and saw how much it amounted to, he hoped he did not have to dig deep to satisfy everyone's curiosity.

"Better skim it off rather than dig," Sanguinetti suggested. "In case there's something there."

Manfredi skimmed. Once, twice, and then the third time the shovel met resistance. Campeau noticed Manfredi's reaction.

"One moment," he said. He stepped in front of Sanguinetti, looked solemnly out at the onlookers, then raised his arms and began apparently to pray. At length. Looks of tolerance adopted when Campeau began were altering into impatience. Manfredi saw Gregory exchange a smile with Sanguinetti.

When Campeau had finished he stepped back, indicating to Manfredi that he might proceed. The pause had given Manfredi time to think of what his spade had encountered.

Now he crouched and began to move dirt away with his hands. Something white came into view. Cloth. There was also a powerful smell.

"What do you think?" he asked Sanguinetti who had crouched beside him. She was slipping on a mask she had taken from her bag.

"Better let me do this."

The cloth was a sheet and the sheet contained a body. The garage doors were raised and Manfredi and Campeau, averting their faces, carried the sagging sheet into the garage and laid it on the floor. Meanwhile, the photographers had rushed into the garage. When Sanguinetti turned back the sheet to reveal the body of Virginia Bauer, it was captured on film for posterity as well as that evening's television audience.

Ambrose

1

Before Basil, before Dowling Hall, there had been home, and waking in the night when the world had died, and he slipped out of bed and pattered barefoot down the hall and tugged at the covers of the big bed until his mother's arm would reach out and sweep him in beside her warm body and sleep came sweetly back again. From Collier Avenue, Ambrose, when he realized what had happened, wanting to shake everyone so they would speak up, clearly, loudly, so a person had half a chance to hear, slipped away among the trees and drove to Alma's.

"Ambrose," she had said, looking at him closely, but she knew, she always knew.

They pulled the shades in her bedroom and she went into the bathroom and came out only when he was in the bed. Then she was beside him, warm, snuggly, crooning like Bing Crosby crooned to Barry Fitzgerald, "tura lura lura, tura lura li, hush my little darling, it's an Irish lullaby." And he slept.

"What is it?" It was night now and she had remained with him; he would have woken if she left the bed.

"They found her."

"Where you said?"

He nodded, face against her breast, her voice echoing in his ear. Suddenly she was scrambling into a sitting position, pushing him away.

"Ambrose, why didn't you say?"

"Say? I told the world."

184

"Oh that! You didn't tell *me*."

"Darling, I did."

"Tell me what happened."

"In the morning."

"Oh Ambrose."

But she lay down again and took him in her arms and soothed him. He was almost asleep again when she spoke while his ear was pressed to her chest. "Ambrose, what will they do to you?"

In the morning, sunlight flooded into the room when she opened the drapes and pulled up the blinds. She was already dressed. She stood at the foot of the bed, pretty as a picture, hands on her hips, frowning at him.

"You said it was Lilian."

"It was!"

"But it was Virginia's body they found. Virginia's."

"Why do you think I came to you?"

2

Captain Manfredi and his faithful man Noonan wanted to know where he had been and failed to be amused when Ambrose told them that a gentleman never tells. It was good that he had gone to Alma, he could not have handled this yesterday in the immediate wake . . . Wrong word, that. Noonan was informing him that he had been seen at Collier Avenue yesterday afternoon. They had been looking for him ever since.

"What is the charge, leaving the scene of an exhumation?"

"This has gone beyond that sort of bullshit, Professor. That was the body of Virginia Bauer we found under the floor of the greenhouse. How did it get there?"

"Aren't you supposed to tell me I should call my lawyer?"

"Would you like to call your lawyer?"

"I don't have one. I would like to make a call though."

He had returned to his rooms from Alma's, showered and dressed and was ready for them when they came. Somewhat unceremoniously, they had driven him off downtown to Manfredi's office. Now the captain pushed a telephone toward Ambrose who dialed Rachel's number.

"Ambrose, where are you?"

"I think I'm arrested."

"I have long thought so. I have been trying to reach you since I heard this astounding news."

"The body in the greenhouse?"

"But Virginia's!"

"A copycat crime, I think is the phrase." He looked over his shoulder at Manfredi, to be sure he caught that. Ambrose had been seeking the phrase all morning, ever since allowing his mind to return to Collier Avenue.

"Where are you?"

"You remember Captain Manfredi? I am in his office. Detective Noonan is here as well. They came for me about an hour ago. I am being grilled."

"Don't say anything."

"Do you know a lawyer?"

"I will bring a lawyer when I come. Remember, not a word."

"I understand."

"Mum's the word."

"I'm an Arrid man myself."

An old joke. He hung up on her laughter.

"I am instructed to say nothing further until Rachel Salma comes with my lawyer."

"Very well, but you can listen."

Manfredi had to get it off his chest. He admitted that he

himself had acted like a damned fool. His excuse was that he'd had no previous experience with people like the Fort Elbow emeriti in retirement at the Residenza. They seemed to occupy the same space/time as everyone else; they spoke the same language, though of course more elegantly. They were more learned. They were on the whole a fascinating, funny, extremely intelligent group of people, no one of whom exhibited what Manfredi would regard as the usual characteristics of a man or woman in his or her seventies. Their sensibility was palpable, they spoke the language of morality and civility, but in their actions they were monsters. Monsters. Exaggerated, the word enabled him to make an appropriate face.

"You all profess to have been devastated by the loss of your friend and Basil Bauer's wife thirty years ago, and then you begin casually talking about having killed her. Basil married a young woman who whatever her background could not possibly have understood what she was getting into. You all turned out for the wedding and it was a memorable festive affair. Did any of you think of her as a human being, a person? Did Basil? Now you have done away with her. Well, by God, I am going to bring you all into the real world this time and you are going to feel its sting."

A B+ performance, Ambrose gauged, really rather good, but he was under instructions, much as he would have liked to say a thing or two by way of rebuttal. He locked his lips and threw away the key. Noonan looked as if he might strike him. Until Rachel arrived, Ambrose felt like a guard at Buckingham Palace being taunted by the tourists as he stared straight ahead, alive but dead, refusing to be distracted. It was a bit of a mystery how a soldier so impervious to his surroundings could possibly guard the queen. Noonan took a turn at flailing Ambrose verbally, and when he was done

Manfredi took up the task again. It was clear they were both quite disgusted with themselves and needed this therapeutic voiding of their psychic bladders.

"Could I go to the bathroom?"

"I'll have to accompany you."

"I am not that sort of person."

"Ho ho."

Ambrose had always had trouble urinating in the presence of others. At Dowling Hall he had used a stall in preference to one of the great white urinals that lined the wall of the washroom, baby showers, as they called them. With the door closed, he was all right, but standing at a urinal it was nothing doing. Why did he think that the boys on either side cared whether or not he did anything? Noonan's presence had the predictable effect.

"Could I use a stall?"

"So you can sit down? I thought you weren't that kind of person."

"I'm going to tell my lawyer about you."

"Look, get it out and get it over with or we're going back."

"We're going back."

In Manfredi's office Noonan interpreted the non-event as one more defiant act on Ambrose's part.

They were saving their best until the lawyer arrived.

3

The lawyer's name was Seymour, his surname, and Rachel called him Mr. Seymour so Ambrose followed suit. Seymour asked to speak to his client alone. When they were alone in a conference room, Seymour said, "Give me a dollar."

Ambrose gave him a dollar. Seymour handed him his card.

"You are my client; I am your lawyer."

They shook hands.

"Now what have they asked you?"

"Well, they want to know why I left after the body was discovered in the greenhouse of Basil's old house on Collier Avenue."

"You were there?"

"Yes."

Seymour's head should have been larger, given the size of his body, the canon of seven was not perfectly exemplified. His hair seemed dyed a kind of mahogany color that went well with his eyes. His dentures were a bad fit, and when he smiled he looked toothless. There was an aroma of cigars.

"I will not ask you why."

"Curiosity."

"Have their questions referred to your admittedly distasteful but innocent claim to have killed Basil Bauer's first wife and buried her in that greenhouse?"

"The phrase copycat killer occurred to me."

"Exactly!" Seymour smiled so intensely that his upper teeth became visible. "A real killing was modeled on an imaginary one." Seymour could not have been more delighted if he had thought of this himself.

Seymour spent a few minutes telling Ambrose what Rachel had told him and asking if it was accurate. By and large it was. The lawyer was satisfied. He stood.

"Now we will ask them to put their money where their mouth is."

Manfredi's manner had been transformed. He was his old emotionless self and Noonan had been relegated to a back wall. Rachel had apparently been trying unsuccessfully to entertain them. Of course she was one of the monsters and could hardly expect decent treatment.

"You may address my client, Captain."

"Did you have anything to do with the death of Virginia Bauer?"

Seymour held up his hand. "Why don't you just ask him to confess to the crime, Captain?"

"Yes. He's good at that."

"Objection."

"Seymour, this is not a courtroom. Your client made a nuisance of himself telling anybody who would listen that thirty years ago he killed Lilian Dahl and buried her under the floor of the greenhouse at her home. Yesterday we called his bluff, removed the floor and uncovered the body of Virginia, the second wife, not the first, of Basil Bauer."

"That is, by taking literally my client's fanciful story you happened to solve another matter that has been puzzling you. For this you are blaming him?"

Good point. Manfredi obviously thought so too. Ambrose was certain that he would soon be on his way, convoyed by Seymour and Rachel. But then Manfredi played a card he must have hoped to hold in reserve.

"I am bringing charges of unlawful entry and theft against Professor Hennessy."

"On what basis?"

"A court order was obtained to search his premises. We found there the notebooks missing from Professor Bauer's office. Fingerprints lifted from items in his bathroom matched fingerprints found at the office."

Seymour did not look at his client. "As I understand that situation, Captain, entry was effected by a key and was not forced."

"That's right. It was idle to try to make it look like forced entry since, if it had been, the security system would have been activated."

"And where would my client have gotten a key?"

"From Knutson, the manager. Ambrose came down some weeks ago, expressed interest in renting an office like that of his good friend Basil Bauer, and was handed a key so he could look around. He went to Woolworth's and made a copy."

"Mr. Woolworth remembered all this of course."

"Hennessy gave the copy to Knutson, a fact he only recently noticed. Putting two and two together, we get the scenario I gave you. But the damning thing is the notebooks."

Seymour could not prevent Ambrose from being charged. While awaiting arraignment Ambrose spent several hours in a cell where he savored the experience. The cellblock was unexpectedly clean, antiseptically clean, but then the jail was new. Ambrose felt that he was locked inside a very well-designed machine. The mirror in his cell was made of shiny metal, the stool was pure porcelain, no seat, the bed had little give and the mattress was firm. Lying on it, staring at the ceiling, Ambrose felt the pain in his back seeping away.

He imagined that this was death row. All appeals had been exhausted, in the streets outside well-meaning people gathered in protest against the death penalty, burning candles, being interviewed by television. How could he explain to them that he deserved to die, that he wanted to die? Their noble sentiments were wasted on him. Perhaps there would be a cable from the Vatican. Spare Professor Hennessy. He has been shriven, he has been given the viaticum, a chaplain would accompany him to the place of execution, reciting one of the penitential psalms, the choice made by the chaplain or by the guest of honor about to be judicially murdered. On the scaffold, Hennessy gave a speech, brief but moving, a defense of capital punishment. What was the world coming to when the malefactor received more sympathy than his victims? Where was the robust Church of old that taught and defended Aquinas's justification of capital punishment? Opposing the death penalty in what the Holy Father had called a culture of death was to cheapen life still further.

The scene became that in *A Man for All Seasons*. A robed Hennessy emerged into the spring sunlight, haggard, pale, but with a new nobility etched in his features. He moved with a firm step toward the block, handed the executioner a sovereign.

"I regret that I have but one sovereign to offer the executioner."

Laughter all around, Ambrose executes a little buck and wing and exits stage right. The executioner joins in the applause. When he removes his mask he is revealed to be Basil. "What a guy!" He shakes his head and wipes away a tear.

"Ambrose Hennessy."

"Yo."

In the Marine Corps he had done ten days in the brig on officer's hours for smashing a window in the barracks when he came home drunk from the slop chute. That was at Miramar in the mountains above San Diego.

"Ambrose Hennessy!"

He was being called again. The turnkey had unlocked his cell electronically and he was being commanded to come forth from prison, as Paul had been summoned by the angel. Soon the whole prison would be automated; they would do away with keepers, keeping only the kept.

He was arraigned before the judge who had married Basil and Virginia. If she remembered him she gave no sign of it. *Sic transit anima mundi.* Bail was set and posted and then finally Ambrose was led away in the custody of Rachel and Mr. Seymour.

4

"What in the world were those notebooks doing in your place?" Rachel wanted to know. Seymour perked up to hear the answer. Ambrose had the feeling that they had been discussing him while he wasted away in his jail cell. During that time the perfect response had occurred to him.

"I suppose I should have taken the precaution of getting a note from Virginia when I took them home. I hadn't known Lilian kept such notebooks. You can imagine how eager I was to read them."

"Virginia let you take those notebooks home?"

"Of course I can't prove that now, can I?"

"That, my dear fellow," said Mr. Seymour, "is a two-way street."

"What about the copy of the key?"

"That was Virginia's suggestion too."

Seymour offered Ambrose a cigar. How often do you get a client like this? Ambrose put it in his pocket for later. "For when you get the charge dismissed."

"A piece of cake."

Manfredi

1

Manfredi went to talk to Alma, to get away from Noonan who was taking unseemly pleasure from the spectacle of Manfredi's unsuccess with Ambrose Hennessy. It would have been too much, perhaps, to prove the man a murderer: it seemed a modest enough aim to nail him for illegal entry and theft. Not without the help of Seymour, no slouch as an advocate of the less than innocent, Ambrose had at least temporarily imported into the real world the aesthetic categories in which he and his cohorts lived. Alma was one of them, of course, but she still seemed a benign case of someone who refuses to accept life on its true terms. The popular lyric as philosophy of life.

"Whoever did this must be punished," Alma said fervently.

"That is your desire; it is my duty."

"Poor, poor Basil."

"Have you spoken with him?"

"For a few minutes. His son Gregory is with him, thank God. A boy without imagination or sense of humor, just what Basil needs."

"I've met him. He lectured me about police work."

"He is a genius at what he does." A little cloud passed across her face. "Most of the time."

"He told me the extent of Basil's wealth."

"Oh?"

194

"Ten million dollars."

"Gosh."

"Give or take a million."

"I'd love to. 'I met a million-dollar baby in the five and ten cent store.' "

She segued into "Sunny Side of the Street" and was soon as rich as Rockefeller.

"I told you he was a whiz."

"His whizdom had nothing to do with it. Basil did this all on his own. You buy blue chips when you're young, hang on to them and live into ripe old age and you're rich. That's the formula."

"Maybe I should have gone to the father rather than the son. But tell me all about Ambrose."

"He whipped my ass. With the help of a lawyer named Seymour recommended by Rachel Salma."

He gave her a brief account of the inspired claim that the dead woman had given Ambrose carte blanche that had let all the air out of his case against the prevaricating professor. What had Basil said to that? "He said it might be so, it very likely was. The son Gregory is less disposed to let bygones be bygones."

"He has never liked Ambrose. Or vice versa. Of course Ambrose never had children."

"He could have been famous."

She hummed a few bars of "My Blue Heaven." "But nothing can really come between Basil and Ambrose. They are two ends of the same thought."

"I won't ask which end Ambrose is."

"But Virginia. She is really and truly dead? I do not want any gory details." She had squeezed her eyes shut and was gripping his arm.

"Absolutely dead."

"How?"

Sanguinetti was preparing the autopsy, her task somewhat complicated by the condition of the body. Alma's eyes squeezed shut again and her grasp on his arm tightened. It seemed reasonable to assume that the cord twisted around Virginia's neck had been the cause of death. Alma was shivering with pity and fear.

"The poor girl. How old was she exactly?"

"Thirty-four."

"My own daughter's age."

That any of these people had children still amazed Manfredi, yet both Basil and Alma did. But Rachel's and Ambrose's somehow seemed the appropriate condition for one seeking to make one's life a work of art, obedient to aesthetic categories only, the whole cultural tradition operating as point of reference in the way that, analogously and corroboratively, tin pan alley did for Alma.

"Whodunnit?"

"I don't know."

"You must have suspects."

"That's why I'm here."

She gave him her Betty Boop expression.

"I want to talk about two authors who have been mentioned, potential biographers who were thwarted by Virginia's getting an inside track on the papers."

"Oh yes."

"Felicia Christman and Ben Ventuti."

"Felicia came to me to ask my help with Basil. A lovely woman. But too much make-up and raven black hair at her age."

"What did she want you to do?"

"She wasn't sure. She was quite theatrical. If she were prevented from writing this biography it would be her death warrant. She had quite a distinguished list of accomplishments."

"How long has it been since you talked with her?"

Alma wasn't sure. Months. Noonan's triumphalism was being put to the test: he was to track down Christman and Ventuti.

"Whatever for?"

"It is a rule of investigation to ask who benefits from the crime."

"Cui bono?"

"Oui, ma chere."

She laughed with delight, lifted his hand to her lips and kissed it. "You could be one of us."

"No threats please."

2

Photographs of Felicia Christman ruled her out as the actual perpetrator of the deed, but the more details gathered about her reaction when Virginia moved into the pole position for the great race to immortality as the biographer of Lilian Dahl, the more plausible it seemed that she might have, perhaps inspired by the increasing number of such cases to attain media fame, hired an assassin to remove the competition. Kneecapping her competitor would not have sufficed unless Felicia herself gained access to the Lilian Dahl papers. When Virginia moved into the matrimonial bed with Basil, Felicia's despondency had turned to despair.

Her case was vastly complicated by the fact that she had represented to her agent and her publisher that she had an inside track with Basil Bauer. She had met with the widower and had no reason to doubt the effect of her charms on the emeritus professor. The jacket photograph on Felicia's most recent books showed her lounging in a negligee on a settee, looking mistily at the potential reader from the depths of her romantic soul. She had essayed poetry in her youth, but recognition and finally acclaim came when she turned to biography, using a novelist's technique to infuse the data with plots and subplots that induced in the reader pity and fear, the emotions appropriate to tragedy, as Aristotle has taught us. For Felicia all lives are tragedies and none more so than those of the women whose lives she imaginatively reconstructed.

"A woman of great sensibility," Basil told Manfredi. "And she felt a spiritual affinity with Lilian. They had been born under the same sign. Libra."

"Ah."

"In fact, I believe she said they shared the same birth date."

"Month and day?"

"Year as well."

Manfredi took another look at the photograph. It had been used on a book published ten years ago; it was a posed shot and thus the subject was the beneficiary of all the artful embellishments and amelioration at the disposal of a good photographer: she did not look like a woman as old as Basil. She had been rebuilt several times and made no bones of her reliance on a clinic in Arizona that negated the effects of time.

Noonan now realized that he and Manfredi would rise or fall together depending on the outcome of the investigation into the murder of Virginia Bauer.

"Murder."

"Premeditated, cold-blooded murder. Impress that on our friends in the press room."

Sanguinetti's report bore this out. Virginia had been strangled with a cord apparently taken from Venetian blinds. The assailant had attacked from the rear: most lesions were on the front of the throat. A bruise in the small of the back suggested that the killer had used his knee to supply a fulcrum, thus increasing the pressure on the throat. Cause of death? Asphyxiation by strangling.

"You said his knee."

"That is inclusive."

"It could have been a woman?"

"Sure," Dr. Sanguinetti said. "If I got the drop on someone and could use my knee like that, I could take out Tarzan."

Dr. Sanguinetti was a petite five six, perhaps 105 to 110 in weight.

"Any sign of sexual molestation?"

She shook her head.

Outside the coroner's office, Manfredi sat behind the wheel of his car and withdrew the report from its envelope. He let his eye travel over the printed form, with the neat entries in Sanguinetti's hand. All in a day's work for her and for him, but her clinical judgments recorded the departure from this vale of tears of Virginia Bauer, gone now to wherever Chip Bufalo had preceded her. All those projections into the future that had animated her actions were severed like the cord that had been used to strangle her.

While Manfredi sat there, Dr. Sanguinetti, in street clothes, came out of the building and hurried across the street to a waiting car. Manfredi was thinking he could give her a citation for street walking when the car into whose passenger seat she had slipped pulled away from the curb. The couple wore the satisfied expressions of young love. The man behind the wheel was Gregory Bauer.

3

Felicia Christman's obituary was discreet, giving no particular reason why death had come to her in Oregon, but then she had gone there for that purpose, taking advantage of one of the lasting benefits of the Third Reich, now rooted in the law of the rainy state. No mention was made of her ruined career, her word discredited with agent and editor. They had dropped her despite the fortunes she had made for them, perhaps certain that she could make no further fortunes now.

"That leaves Ben Ventuti," Noonan said unnecessarily.

The man who had made a living swiftly composing manuscripts that had the look at least of books, authoring, as he put it, in mere weeks bios of rock stars, Formula 1 race car drivers, and a Manhattan madame whose plea for a return to biblical ethics and family values had caused a bleep in the book's run on the way to the paperback edition. *Jezibel Says. . . .* had sold forty thousand copies in hard back and got an unrealistic advance from Ball Books for reprint rights. They brought it out with another lurid title on pederast priests, authored by Sy Spiega, one of Ben's pseudonyms. The promotional line—"If One Ball is Good . . ."—proved a winner and both books, studded with photos, sold like popcorn.

He was currently in Fort Wayne, Indiana, mere miles away, researching another Spiega book. His agent took the bait when Noonan told him that the woman who had been going to do the official Lilian Dahl book was dead, and gave the number of the motel where Ben was holed up. Noonan and Manfredi drove to Fort Wayne.

The manager of the Ho Hum hadn't seen Ventuti for days but he was still at work in the motel. What might have caused legal problems, grabbing at the cleaning girl when she showed up at his room that morning, had been smoothed over when he told the girl she was the spitting image of Madonna and that lunging at her as he had was part of the research for the book he was doing. He showed her his computer. He gave her a signed copy of *Jezibel Says*. . . . He got her to sign a release so he could use that morning's episode in his book.

When Manfredi and Noonan knocked on the door of 212 they were prepared to meet a resourceful person. Their knock was not answered. They used the key they had gotten from the manager. Ventuti was sprawled on the bed, the room reeked of bourbon, the battery on his computer had run down.

Noonan had experience with a drunken uncle and proved to be an effective soberer. Step one was to pick Ventuti up and carry him to the bathroom and dump him in the tub. Step two was to prop him up so that he hung over the toilet. A powerful emetic brought up everything Ventuti had in him. Flush, back into the tub, pull the curtain, turn on the shower. Beyond the curtain, a cursing, terrified Ventuti came to life, convinced he was drowning and trying to get to the surface. Step three was to towel him down, calm him, and give him a shot of bourbon. Step four was coffee, lots of it.

"He's yours," Noonan said.

"Who the hell are you guys?" Ventuti's bloodshot eyes rolled from one to another.

"Jezibel sent us."

But he didn't really remember Jezibel. He had written thirteen books since then. No wonder he drank. The man was a menace.

"When did you leave Fort Elbow?"

The bloodshot eyes rolled to port and back again.

"You will remember Lilian Dahl."

Through the mists of his mind and memory connection was made. "The poet. 'Gone glimmering now, yesterday . . .' No, that's the other woman poet."

"And Virginia Hardie."

But only two bloodshot eyes looked up.

"The biographer of Lilian Dahl."

"That bitch."

"Lilian?"

"The other one. She aced me out. I swore I'd kill her."

"She's dead."

"What?"

"Someone killed her."

"The hell you say."

"The woman you threatened to kill is dead. You're conveniently located here a few miles away. You hop in your car, drive to Fort Elbow. . . ."

Ben Ventuti was laughing, a not quite sober but cheerful laugh. Manfredi and Noonan waited until he was through. The bloodshot eyes swam in tears from the laughing.

"You don't know I can't walk, do you? I have to use that thing."

He pointed and for the first time they noticed the little electrical cart in the corner. Ventuti's car was rigged so that he could be lifted into it in his electric chair and transfer to the driver's seat where pedals had been turned into handles. He was mobile enough, but it was hard to see him descending from his vehicle in the electric cart at Basil's office, effecting entry and all the rest.

"Go ahead, arrest me. I could use the publicity."

Noonan asked him where he had been the previous weekend.

"That may have been one I lost. Check with the manager here."

The weekend desk clerk had seen Ventuti's car in the lot both Saturday and Sunday.

Ventuti called after them when they left. "Have they assigned a new writer yet?"

4

Prentiss at the lab regarded all calls on his professional services as an imposition. He loved to be called to court to testify, but the prosecutor avoided him like sin. Not only was he boring, he had a voice that rose like a belch from some subbasement of his soul. He had a large head, wore his hair to his shoulders and had a pouter pigeon chest. He glared at Manfredi.

"Virginia Bauer."

"How are you? I'm Walter Prentiss."

"Keep that up and you'll get your own show. You ready to testify on that sheet and cord?"

"On the sheets I'll do anything." He swung away and propelled himself across his working area in his chair. He seldom got out of the chair, perhaps because standing up robbed him of authority. He was perhaps five three in Cuban heels, embargo or no embargo. He pulled an oversized envelope from a drawer and wheeled back. He removed the sheet from the envelope. It was stained with the body fluids that had been released as Virginia exited this life.

"This could have come from anywhere. It was manufactured in Mexico but marketed here. The type is that favored by hotels and motels since it can survive hundreds of washings."

"Don't hotels and motels have an identification on their linens?"

"Many do. Not all. It may not have come from a hotel, you understand."

"And the cord?"

"It helps that it comes with the plastic handle still on it." Prentiss held up a white plastic thimble-like object and shook from it the knotted end of the grayish cord. "These were customized by Francois Decorations." He let Manfred see that legend impressed in the plastic.

Francois. That name and the gray motif took Manfredi to the office Virginia and Basil had rented near the mall. Knutson was in his office, standing on his head in a corner. He righted himself and smiled sheepishly.

"Yoga."

He came along with Manfredi to the office and opened the door. The first blind cord he examined had a plastic cup of the kind Prentiss had shown him. Francois Decorations.

"What are we looking for?" Knutson asked.

"The cord that isn't here."

Knutson found the relevant blind. "Hey, this one doesn't have a cord."

It was Manfredi's impulse to dismantle the blind and carry it down to the lab, but that would not be going by the book. He called Prentiss and told him he had a blind date for him.

The cord used to strangle Virginia had come from a blind in her office. Manfredi stayed there and told Prentiss to phone him the verdict. It could have happened right here. Someone could have come up from behind as she sat at her desk, dropped the cord over her head and jerked it back. She tries to rise, pushing at the desk and then the assailant gets his knee into her back and it is all over. Nothing the lab had picked up before provided physical evidence that that is what had happened. But wherever it had been done the assailant had used a cord taken from this office. That narrowed the field and brought a grim smile to Manfredi's face. He picked up the phone and called Noonan.

"Bring in Hennessy."

"He's out on bail."

"This is a new charge. First degree murder."

"Where are you going?"

"Out to the Residenza to examine a sheet."

Basil

1

When Rachel had recounted the way in which her friend Seymour had rescued Ambrose from the snares of his own imaginings, Gregory was furious.

"Illegal entry and theft! A woman has been killed."

"They got Al Capone for failure to pay his income tax."

Gregory groaned. "Don't mention taxes when I'm on vacation."

Basil reacted to this description of Gregory's sojourn with his father at this time of great tragedy. "Vacation?"

"I had to tell my clients something."

"Ambrose has explained that Virginia gave him a key and told him he could take Lilian's notebooks home to read. He made a copy of the key as a convenience."

"She had no right to give anyone a key."

Basil looked at Gregory. "She had as much right as I do."

It was Rachel who called to tell Basil the new news about Ambrose.

"Basil, I am beginning to think he did do it."

"Nonsense."

"The sheet is from here. The sheet they found her in came from the Residenza."

Basil handed the phone to Gregory and wandered off to his bedroom where he sat in the shaded dark and wondered how long it would be before he himself was dead. He was already finding it difficult to summon a vivid image of Virginia.

It was far easier to conjure up from memory the face of Lilian. How sad she'd had so short a life. He could see now what nonsense it was to imagine that she had run away. In Omaha, Dr. Hardie was now in his way a widower too, the wife he had put away gone definitively from him now, no matter that he had ached to have her back. Basil had lost two wives and it grieved him that the losses left him all but unmarked, inside, in his heart. Not even Lilian had been able, when remembered, to bring him to tears, to helpless wrenching weeping. With others he could summon the words and gestures, the moist eyes, the tremor in the voice. It took so very little to play the public role of abject widower. But alone before the mirror he saw only his old self and his eyes were dry.

There was, as he had learned, positive pleasure to be had from savoring the pastness of the past. Oh, to lament the *dies ante acta,* what once was and is no more, but such sweet sorrow is a present experience and the past it feeds on is without real sting. Was that not the essential message of Proust?

"Half Jew, half Catholic," Ambrose said, knowing all about it. " 'It was my shame and now it is my boast,'—Belloc—I read the whole of *A la recherche* in French. I have shown you the lovely edition of the *Bibliotheque de la Pleiade* that I have worn out as if it were a breviary. Basil, I even read *Jean Santeuil.* Dear God, forgive this boasting. It is as if one were to preen himself on having read *Stephen Hero* as well as *Portrait of the Artist.*"

"*Stephen Hero.*"

"Basil, there should be an international law binding everywhere preventing publishers and/or heirs of writers from bringing out what the writers were wise enough to file away. Poor Hemingway."

"You were speaking of Proust."

"Ah, the smell of fresh baked pastry. For you and me it is the smell of spring at Dowling Hall, the voices of picnickers coming to us from across the lake as we lay in our dormitory beds."

"Cast-off condoms found by the burnt-out fires."

Ambrose, of course, was right. For either of them those times, now sixty years in the past, were more real than any present could ever be: they were their real present. And all the things attaching to those years partook of the same reality.

It was at Dowling Hall that Ambrose had learned to turn failure into moral superiority.

2

The kitchen girl, just seventeen years old, was pulled from Lake Susanna on a morning in May, 1942, their senior year. Her name was Maureen and her thin black hair fanned out from her head as she lay in the water, her pale skin paler now and the freckles faded as if the time the body had been in the water had begun to wash them away. She had come ashore below the power plant, which was near the shore, but it was thought she had entered the water from the dock farther up, not far from the kitchen door. Like the other kitchen girls, she boarded in a dormitory located in a wing off the kitchen, where the nuns kept an eye on them because the students kept an on eye on the girls.

"Would she have intended to swim?"

"In her best dress?"

"She didn't know how to swim. She was terrified of the water."

"She went to meet someone," a thin voice said.

"Who?"

The other girls didn't know or wouldn't say.

Ambrose knew and didn't say, nor did Basil who knew what Ambrose knew. They had vied with one another to catch the attention of Maureen.

"I am resolved not to leave this school a virgin, Basil."

"The school or yourself."

"How would you put it?"

"As a virgin I am resolved not to leave this school? No. I am resolved that when I leave this school I shall not be a virgin."

"That's it."

"I don't think males are called virgins."

"What then?"

"Uninitiated."

"That will do."

They were both influenced by the scene in Anthony Adverse, where the mulatto woman taking a barrel bath espies the young boy and initiates him.

And Maureen, as innocent as they, had been chosen to share the passage of one of them into the ranks of the initiated. They were prepared for a long campaign, rivalry, small victories, setbacks, pressing on, but always with the threat that nothing could be accomplished before graduation.

Ambrose said, "I want to confess the sin here at school."

In a confessional in the crypt below the school chapel a yawning friar listened to their peccadilloes and waved them away with an absolution. Lulled into complacency by the redundancy of solitary sins, the friar would be jolted awake by such a feat as this.

"That is presumption."

"That I will sin or that I will have the opportunity to confess?"

Basil tried to catch Maureen's eye in the kitchen, making

unnecessary trips there during meals, but she gave him no encouragement. In a stroke of inspiration, Ambrose wrote her a note, risking interception but eager to take the risk. Discovery itself had attractions: he would acquire a reputation for leading a clandestine life. On the other hand, if she answered, he was certain the rest would be as easy as sin. She answered. They arranged to meet during evening study hall when Ambrose could ask permission to go to the library. He would slip out the side door, she would slip out the kitchen door, they could talk on the playing field beyond. And they did. Ambrose described the look of the lighted study hall from that vantage-point, at such an hour with a girl clinging to his arm, and Basil tingled with jealousy at the tale.

The unexpected happened. They fell in love. Seduction gave way to a mindless devotion. Basil pointed out that while undeniably female and vaguely pretty, Maureen was an unlikely object of a grand passion. They had so little in common.

"We have the great common denominator in common."

"Do you even kiss her?"

"Please."

"Or feel her breasts?"

Ambrose turned away. But the questions put him back on the right track, the right track being the wrong one. Meetings with Maureen became friendly tussles in which she halfheartedly fended him off. He pressed for a longer meeting. These ten or fifteen minute sessions on the playing field no longer sufficed. They arranged to meet after lights out.

This was daring indeed. Any boy caught out of his bed after lights out was immediately under suspicion of wrongdoing. What this might be was unclear to most, but Ambrose was reading Proust in translation and thought he knew. When he finished the last volume, he recommended that the librarian remove them from the shelves.

"You're the only one who has ever checked them out."

"May I be the last," Ambrose said piously.

Ambrose would creep from the dormitory and descend three flights of steps to a side door. He could exit by this door, but if it closed tightly he could not open it from the outside. As a precaution, he undid the lock on one of the windows in the basement lavatory. Maureen would execute a similar departure from the kitchen girls' dorm. They would walk along the path that bordered the lake. Ambrose sighed. The rest he must leave to Basil's imagination.

Basil was a good loser. There was a sense in which he felt a participant in the adventure. Indeed, he cast himself in the role of secret sharer. Five minutes after Ambrose crept out of the dormitory and the stairway door was eased shut behind him, Basil followed. He had chosen a spot earlier, one that both concealed him and gave him a good view of the lakeside path. He headed directly to his post.

He saw what happened on the dock. He saw the kind of friendly tussle Ambrose had described begin but finally Maureen yielded and Ambrose held and kissed her. It was a brief kiss. It ended with Maureen pushing Ambrose away. At least that must have been her intention. But Ambrose was firmly planted on the narrow dock. In pushing him, Maureen pushed herself backward, she lost her balance and her arms began a windmill churning. There was a splash as she fell into the water, a minute of awful threshing and crying out and then silence. Ambrose stood a solitary figure on the dock. Where there had been two, now there was one. Ambrose seemed to be frozen where he stood. Then he turned and ran back toward the school.

Had Maureen told the other girls of her adventure?

Had they perhaps crowded to a window and watched

those assignations on the playing field?

Had she confided in anyone about her late night rendez-vous with Ambrose?

Would the note Ambrose had written be discovered?

The two friends suffered through days of agony, wondering what the answer to these questions might be. Of course, Ambrose was not concerned when he learned that Basil knew.

"You saw what happened?"

"Yes."

"Everything?"

"She lost her balance and fell in."

"I mean before."

Had Basil seen him kiss Maureen? That was what Ambrose wanted to know. Neither of them mentioned his failure to do anything to rescue the poor girl after she had fallen into the lake. Her friends were to say that she could not swim. The water into which she had fallen was four feet deep. She could have walked ashore, but of course she panicked. And Ambrose did nothing and then ran away and said nothing. The first period of agony was the day-and-a-half before three freshmen noticed the body and spread the alarm.

"I will love her always," Ambrose said.

With the passage of time an idealized version of Maureen dominated Ambrose's references to her. But he did not object when Basil gave a more accurate description.

"Joyce had his Nora Barnacle, I had my Maureen."

"You were cheated out of a dramatic confession."

"Oh I went to confession."

"What did you confess?"

"Murder."

3

"Gregory, it was good of you to come. I cannot tell you how much I appreciate your visit, but you must get back to your own life."

"I think I'll stay a little longer, Dad."

"But your clients."

"A computer with a modem, a phone, a fax, and my office is wherever I am."

"But can you keep your mind on it?"

"Sometimes that doesn't help. Besides, look at how well you've done." He laid a hand on his father's arm. "Phyllis is coming for the funeral."

Another reason for Gregory's staying turned out to be the young pathologist, Sara Sanguinetti.

"She performed the autopsy on Virginia."

"Good heavens."

"The killer will be found," she assured Basil. She was a lovely birdlike young woman, obviously taken by Gregory and, it appeared, vice versa, too.

"Haven't you heard the story of my mother?"

Basil intervened. "She wasn't killed, Gregory."

Psychiatry is nonsense, of course, but sometimes Basil wondered if what had happened to his mother had turned Gregory away from marriage. His interest in Sara was welcome. At the Residenza, having a drink with Ambrose, he mentioned the liaison.

"Your son wanted my head."

"He thinks you're guilty."

"Of what?"

"Does it matter?"

"It matters to me when he stirs up the police. I will never

forget the hours I spent behind bars—in a thoroughly modern, utterly inhuman cell. Basil, may you never have a similar experience."

The episode was becoming part of Ambrose's standard repertoire, and Basil listened as he perfected the account. It would soon rival the vicissitudes of St. Paul, which the apostle himself recalled for a somewhat different purpose than Ambrose. Ambrose was less inclined to dwell on why the charges had been dropped, since it was difficult not to give some credit to Mr. Seymour who apparently was dining out on the story.

"He has become an utter bore about it," Rachel said when she joined them. "He has no sense of story, of how suspense is created, of the role of peripety and chance."

"He really shouldn't be using my material."

"He did get you off, Ambrose."

"I believe the epiphany was mine, Rachel."

"You mean when you remembered how Virginia gave you a key?"

"And she also agreed when I asked to take the notebooks home." Ambrose looked her directly in the eye.

"You have never mentioned their contents."

"Basil, they are fascinating. Absolutely fascinating. Is it too late to observe that Lilian was a woman of extraordinary talent? What a tragedy that she was taken from us so soon. Surely you know the notebooks, Basil."

"I never read them. Aren't they like a diary?"

"They are like and unlike a dozen things. Perhaps the *Papirer* of Kierkegaard offers the closest parallel. I have come to think that it was when she was confiding in these notebooks that her genius reached its finest flower. An *apercus*, a simile dashed off and then, pages later, returned to. And the range of her reading! She could pin and place a writer with a phrase. To whom do you suppose 'the whalebone of an ass' refers?"

They gave up.

"Edith Wharton."

"What does it mean?"

"Think about it."

Ambrose had been pleasantly surprised to finds *mots* of his own recorded. He found the practice beyond reproach. She gave credit and she was not writing for publication.

"I won't ask what she says about me," Rachel said.

"Very well."

"I will ask! What does she say?"

"You must read them yourself. I have come upon some rather catty references to myself, and I must say I prefer to have been the first to find them."

"You're not erasing things, are you?"

"Lilian always wrote in ink," Basil said.

"And you and I in water."

Was he thinking perhaps of Maureen?

Manfredi

1

Phillips, the undertaker, was not a friend Manfredi had made in the course of his professional work, although many objects of his attention as a detective had provided unscheduled opportunities for such as Philips. Manfredi had met Philips at the Knights of Columbus.

"Columbus was Italian," Manfredi explained, when eyebrows lifted. He was happy that questioners did not consider him the kind of person who liked strange costumes and quasi-religious ritual.

"So are the Sons of Italy."

"I am one of those as well," he said, crossing his fingers, referring quite literally to his origins. His people had come from a province in southern Italy called Basilicata, a coincidence that had preyed on his mind often of late as he became more enmeshed in the machinations of the emeriti ensconced at the Residenza.

"Of course," Basil said, when asked if he knew of it. "It was part of Magna Graecia, the name is an adjective of Greek origin, meaning royal, regal, noble. Basil of course means king."

"I thought you were a herb," Rachel said.

"That's my uncle."

"You said you'd never say it."

"I'll say uncle for you anytime, sweetheart."

Rachel laughed explosively, Basil melodiously, Manfredi merely smiled, along for the ride. He had come to ask discreetly, it was no business of his, if arrangements had been made for Virginia's burial. He was to learn that the little group prided themselves on the thoroughness and panache with which they bade farewell to friends.

"Not that, God forbid, we would presume to twist the liturgy to our purposes or encourage people to ascend to the pulpit and disgorge exquisitely tasteless paeans of praise, with the deceased playing a decidedly secondary role to the loquacious lamenter. No this is over and above and *entre nous*."

It would be held in the common room of the Residenza. Alma was in charge. The funeral itself had been put into the capable hands of—Basil consulted a slip on his desk—Downey Phillips.

"You got me," Phillips had said. "For all I know they just opened the Yellow Pages and let their fingers do the walking."

"Will it take place here?"

"Here" was the vast complex done in a species of colonial architecture that housed Philips's thriving business. "My father owed a saloon. He didn't drink himself, but he reasoned others always would, in good times or in bad, to celebrate or for consolation. I carried the principle a step further. Everyone has to die."

"As long as you don't do it yourself, you can cash in."

"I would not have put it quite that way."

The funeral would not take place in Phillips's Funeral Home. Nor would it take place at St. Barnabas, the parish in which the Residenza was located. Father Herrick of the campus Newman Club had urged that Virginia be buried from his chapel.

"As a convenience to her many friends in the faculty and student body."

"I wouldn't want anything . . ." Basil began. How to describe the shenanigans in the Center chapel? No need to. Herrick had closed his eyes and raised a hand.

"I understand. *De gustibus* and all that."

This response became legend at the Residenza. Basil and Ambrose developed a dialogue between the bereaved and Father Herrick that featured the chaplain's malapropism and was salted with others, a veritable *catena aurea* of clichés: Let sleeping dogs lie. Beauty is only skin deep. Nature abhors a vacuum but dust to dust. Far from being dissuaded by this from having Virginia buried from the Newman Chapel, Basil now would have insisted upon it, anticipating a feast of the inapposite.

Manfredi saw no reason to acquaint Phillips with the quirks and foibles of the emeriti. He no longer spoke of them at home to Teresa. In the privacy of his own mind he balanced incredulity and the indubitable evidence of his eyes and ears.

"Here is what in my estimation captures the very essence of the comic." Ambrose's eyes widened and he fixed them on his listener. "A man is caught in bed with another woman by his wife. He sits naked on the edge of the bed where the floozie all *membra disiecta* still lies and he denies everything. 'Who are you going to believe, me or the evidence of your senses?' " Ambrose laughed as if hearing himself tell it for the first time. He called it a Cartesian joke, then stopped.

"Like anything that is what it is, it requires no explanation."

Like the emeriti, perhaps.

2

"Where's the chapel?"

"This is it."

Manfredi had thought it was a classroom. But then he noticed the banner on the far wall, an amateurish thing on which Peace and Love and God spelled with letters cut crudely from different colored cloth were sewn haphazardly.

"A gift of the Homeless Center," the priest said.

"Ah."

"I should tell you that I often preach against police brutality, particularly as manifested in homophobia."

"We can't have too much of that."

The chaplain smiled and then frowned.

"You will be preaching at the Virginia Bauer funeral?"

"Yes, yes. Do we know yet who was responsible?"

"No, Father."

"Jim."

"It is not unlikely, Jim, that when you preach at the funeral Mass, the murderer will be in the audience."

"My gawd." He covered his mouth with his hand and looked wide-eyed over his fingertips at Manfredi.

"That is why I and my assistant will be here. I understand that you regularly tape services."

"The system is built in. It is simultaneously shown on monitors in the social rooms."

"The overflow audience?"

"No. No. I don't like to make a big thing of worship, as if it is something foreign. I tell the kids to go on doing what they're doing. Of course they can't resist a television screen."

"You can see what I'm getting at, Jim."

"No, I don't."

"If we could have a copy of that tape . . ."

He backed away from Manfredi as if the captain had engaged in police brutality.

"I could do nothing to deliver anyone over to our so-called criminal justice system, Captain Manfredi."

"Egidio."

"What?"

"That's my name. Egidio."

"They baptized you that?"

Manfredi held his peace. He wanted that tape. In the end, he gave Jim the promise that Egidio Manfredi would do everything he could to see that the prosecutor did not seek the death penalty for anyone to whose arrest and conviction the Newman Center video led.

3

Noonan had devised a chart summarizing where they were in the investigation of the death of Virginia Bauer.

Friday, about 9 a.m.—Virginia last seen by Basil.

Saturday, between 6 and midnight—estimated time of death.

Cause of death: asphyxiation by strangulation with a cord cut from Venetian blind at Virginia/Basil office.

Sheet in which body was wrapped of the same make and texture as those used at the Residenza.

Sunday evening—Basil at Residenza for McMullin celebration.

Monday, 9:20 a.m.—911 call by Basil to report Virginia missing.

Manfredi's eyes drifted from the monitor. The chronology must indicate where all the principals were during the Triduum, Rachel, Alma, Basil . . . And there was the son as well, Gregory, when had he arrived? However attractive the prospect of having a neatly annotated time line undoubtedly was, producing it was going to be a task. Should he assign it to Noonan? What he decided was to procrastinate. How like the emeriti he was becoming.

Alma

1

There had been a memorial service for Lilian, not the creative commemoration that Ambrose later arranged as what he called a more commensurately cultural response to the loss of our dear friend, but a religious service at the Newman Club. The chaplain in those days was a distinguished priest who had taught in Rome, had written a sympathetic book on W. G. Ward, Newman's nemesis, was culturally incompatible with the then raw extension campus, but a favorite of Basil and Ambrose. The Very Reverend Monsignor Hugh Jameson. On duty, he always wore his monsignorial cassock with its red piping, redolent as he had put it of *una speranza episcopale*. Monsignor Jameson came to the later commemoration arranged by Ambrose, but the service at the Newman Center was conducted according to the ritual and rubrics then in force. Vatican II had yet to turn the Mass into a liturgy that descended degree by degree into the banality of the ordinary. Lilian's funeral Mass was in Latin; Monsignor Jameson wore black vestments, the *Dies Irae* was sung, solo, by Jameson, and those who followed the English translation in their St. Andrew's Missals could shudder at the unrelenting picture of ultimate judgment and the possibility of eternal punishment.

"People think Dante made it up," Ambrose said. "But read the letter to Can Grande della Scala."

Jameson nodded. He had seemed not quite to trust Ambrose, and the fact that Jameson too had gone to

Dowling Hall did not entirely remove the slight chill. They had been of different generations, of course, and had not been contemporaries at the school. Still it was a shared formative experience. Did Jameson see in Ambrose what he might have become if he had not turned to the priesthood, a large frog in a small pond, pontificating on a campus that threw open its welcoming arms in the manner of the lines on the Statue of Liberty? Give me your ungifted, your dull, your huddled masses looking for a boost up the economic ladder. It was *de rigueur* for Fort Elbow faculty to think of their employment as a joke they were playing on their earlier ambitions.

How could Latin be a dead language if it had been used daily for two millennia in the Church? Ambrose oddly did not complain when worse English translation followed bad, down the scale to banality, that is, to the living language as commonly heard. Why didn't they use the translation of the Bible Ronald Knox had made, fulfilling an ambition of Newman himself?

"Evelyn Waugh said that it would be the standard translation used in our churches for centuries ahead."

"Waugh was no prophet." Jameson added, "A Waugh profiteer?"

"Knock, knock."

"Knox?"

There were moments when Jameson seemed ready to cross the line and become one of them. But it never really happened. Perhaps it was the long discipline of liturgical Latin that prevented jazz-like improvisation. When the breviary became the Liturgy of the Hours, Jameson received permission to continue with the *Breviarium Romanum*, which he had begun to read daily as a subdeacon and did not intend to abandon now.

They were to remember Jameson wistfully as they suffered through the New Age antics of Father Jim.

2

Rachel was with Ambrose, each with their nose in a notebook, which is why Alma had dropped by. Ambrose nodded toward the pile on his coffee table. The notebooks were spread over the table's surface, several irregular piles, two had slid onto the floor, all identical. Alma could not believe that this mass of words was only a fraction of what Lilian had left behind, these notebooks kept a secret from them all, even apparently from Basil.

They were distinguished from one another only by the dates printed in the white square on the marbled black cover. Alma randomly picked 21.x.59-31.i.60 and opened it. Was it from Mortimer Adler that she had learned first to leaf through a book, acquaint herself with its contents, and only then, knowing roughly what you were getting into, begin, following the Aristotelian principle, from the generic to the specific, the vague to the precise.

Flesh of my flesh, bone of my bone. A husband cannot be that but children are. Literally, spelled from the alphabet of my body, severed words over which I have little control. Mothers love their children. Ambrose would call this a per se notum *proposition. Basil says it is only* ut in pluribus. *There are exceptions. How strange children are.*

I named Phyllis, Basil named Gregory. We both chose Greek names. In Italian an illiterate person is called analfabetico. *If knowledge of the Greek alphabet were the criterion . . .*

In the winter there is snow on the fields.

and pursuing hunters move through cold . . .

The unrelieved anapest bores while the iambic line gambols on forever without calling attention to itself. Or is this merely the influence of Shakespeare.

I pray that Phyllis will be plain and simple, ordinary in the best sense. Kierkegaard described himself as a letter set backward in a line. How enviable all the others, looking the right way. Which is Gregory?

Whenever the mind is like to roam
over the hills and dales of home
it will discover the secret name
that guarantees each thing's the same.

That was awful. Yeats wrote fifteen lines of poetry every day. Eliot composed on a typewriter. How much did they keep?

And then, flipping the pages, Alma found this: *Guess who's expecting? Alma mater.*

Manfredi

1

"The doctor called again," Gloria said.

"See if you can reach her."

Sara Sanguinetti, the petite pathologist. She had called when he was out and when he tried to reach her she was gone. There was a note from Phillips, the undertaker, as well. A pretty lugubrious list.

"No one answers there," Gloria called.

"Try again later."

He himself called Phillips, it might be personal. A great deal on a burial plot for an old buddy, a bargain on cremations? A fire sale.

Someone with a sepulchral voice answered and told him to wait.

"Phillips."

"Manfredi."

A pause. "Egidio, could you come over here."

"What's up?"

"Maybe you can tell me."

When he got there, they went to Phillips' office where the undertaker carefully shut the door.

"What's the problem?"

"The body dug up on Collier."

"Virginia Bauer?"

"That's the problem."

He wanted to make an odd suggestion, and there weren't

225

many people Phillips would be as frank about this as he could be with Egidio. After all, an undertaker's reputation is everything; lose that and forget it. Manfredi let him take all the time he needed. It seemed that one of Phillip's assistants questioned the identification of the body.

"Come on."

"She knew the woman, she took some classes at the local campus, and she tells me this isn't her."

"The body we dug up is not Virginia Bauer?"

"I know, I know. You were there. The son identified the body; that was required. But this girl is insistent."

"Whose body is it?"

Phillips shrugged. "She's sticking with whose it isn't."

Manfredi was trying to laugh this off and get out of there, but he found himself recalling the scene in the greenhouse in as much detail as he could. The dirt was cleared away, Sara Sanguinetti knelt and pulled back the sheet. The blond hair and then immediately the cord around the neck and, be honest, he shut his eyes.

"It looks like the wrong wife."

Who said that? Sanguinetti. But that hadn't been the identification that counted. Gregory Bauer had done the official identification.

Phillips repeated that, just to put his mind at rest. "I mean, think of it, Egidio, I can't bury the wrong body. I telephoned Dr. Sanguinetti."

"Why?"

"To see if she could give me reassurance as to the identification of the body. Why her? I wanted something scientific."

"What did she say?"

"She will see what she can do."

"Like?"

"Sometimes people store blood, their own blood, in case

they ever have an operation and need a transfusion. This is to eliminate the risk of anything, you know."

"Had Virginia done that?"

"No. But she had a physical before she got married. Dr. Sanguinetti was going to see if the tests might provide a basis for allaying my doubts."

"Have you heard from her?"

"Not yet."

"She's been calling me."

"I wish she'd call me."

They sat in silence for a while. Manfredi said, "Who all has seen the body?"

"No one. It's not a pretty sight. The family does not want an open casket wake."

"Then Basil has seen the body?"

"No."

"Gregory?"

"Would you care to . . ."

Manfredi nodded and they got up. They descended a spiral staircase into the room where grim arts were practiced. The air was cold, the smells strange and repugnant. Like an obscene altar a table stood starkly alone in the center of the room, covered with a rubber sheet. Various instruments were suspended above the table, in easy reach of the workman. Manfredi was relieved to see that the table was empty.

Think of it as the morgue. It was just one step along from the setting in which Sara Sanguinetti plied her trade. There was a wall in which, as at the morgue, bodies were filed away. Phillips who seemed more animated in this setting, went to a drawer and pulled it open. Not the shrouded contents Sanguinetti might display. The woman was dressed and her hair made ready.

"We stopped right here when we learned there wouldn't be a viewing."

But Manfredi was looking at the body. He came to the side of the drawer, so that he could see the face better. But as in the greenhouse his eyes went to the throat.

"I could have fixed that better," Phillips said defensively.

"Who is she?"

"Don't you know?"

"I never saw her before in my life."

"It isn't Virginia Bauer?"

"When you first pulled out the drawer, looking at the top of the head, seeing the blond hair, I thought so. Your assistant is right. That's not Virginia."

"Oh my God."

2

The task of talking with Basil devolved on Manfredi, as well it should. While he himself had not identified the body dug up from beneath the greenhouse floor on Collier Avenue as Basil's missing second wife, he had acquiesced. He had wanted to get out of the confining space, the heat, all those people looking in as if this were a performance done for their sake. None of them could have gotten a good, confirming look when Sara Sanguinetti opened the sheet to reveal the blonde within.

They had carried the body in the sheet into the garage and Manfredi had left it to the pathologist and her helpers. He himself went outside and around the house, away from the crowd, and took gulping breaths of air. He was certain that he would throw up, but he didn't. He didn't even want to think these excuses now, permit them to form in his mind. This was inexcusable. For two days they had permitted Basil to think they had discovered his missing wife.

Manfredi pressed the ball of his thumb against his lower lip. They still did not know what had happened to Virginia Bauer. Could that be his approach to Basil? Professor, for all we know your wife is still alive. He decided that he wanted to speak to Gregory first. The son had relieved his father of the unsavory tasks associated with the discovery of the body. He had been too hasty in making the identification in order to expedite matters.

Gregory was not at his father's apartment.

"Can I take a message, Captain?"

"Thank you, professor." Meaning, no thank you. He did not hang up immediately, waiting to see if he might impulsively tell Basil what had to be classified as good news. But Basil hung up before Manfredi could say anything more.

A double whammy. He had been teased into tearing up the floor of the greenhouse because of Ambrose Hennessy's stupid story about having buried Lilian Dahl there thirty years ago. Result: the discovery of a fresh body. Manfredi could have identified her correctly; he had spoken to Virginia. He had, as she claimed, harassed her over the death of Chip Bufalo. He had become a sufficient authority. And that authority had apparently been exercised when he hurried away from the scene after they had carried the sheeted body into the garage and laid it on the floor.

But Virginia had not been Virginia. The clownish appearance of the corpse only half made up by Phillips's staff rendered identification more difficult.

"I am going to suggest something that I will deny I ever said."

"Go ahead."

"Get me some good photos. I'll make her look like his wife."

"What's the point if there's no viewing?"

"For our sakes."

Partners in crime. They might make a habit of it.

"Deny you ever said that."

"Okay. Okay."

He phoned Noonan and told him to go find Gregory Bauer and bring him to Phillips's Funeral Home.

"What's up?"

"Later." But it's what would be down that was the question now.

While he was at it, he telephoned the lab. It would be well to have a representative of the coroner here when they explained it all to Gregory. The phone rang and rang. Manfredi imagined the sound of the ringing trying every corner of the room. How many extensions rang at once? It was enough to wake the dead.

Later the phone on Phillips's desk rang. He snatched it up.

"Good. Good. Send him in." He put down the phone. "Mister Bauer." He seemed to be imitating his receptionist.

A tap on the door. Manfredi got up and opened it, but Phillips was standing beside him, washing his hands with air, when he pulled back the door and Basil Bauer stood there.

3

"I thought you were your son," Phillips yelped.

"That is a metaphysical feat of which I am incapable. I have come to see the body. It is cowardly of me to hold back."

"You want to see the body?"

"Yes."

"She isn't ready yet."

Manfredi looked at Phillips and the undertaker shut up.

"I don't want to see her after you have done your work. It

is time I faced up to what has happened."

"I will come with you," Manfredi said.

Let Basil see for himself the mistake that had been made, then they would discuss what to do. He took comfort from the thought that Basil had come to fulfill a grisly duty and would find that, possibly, just possibly, he was not yet a two-time widower.

Down into the cold they went, Basil descending the spiral staircase carefully.

"Will we find the circle of ice below?"

"The temperature is a constant 35 degrees."

"Ice would melt. Satan would be set free."

Anything that helped get him through this ordeal, Manfredi supposed.

At the foot of the stairway, they lined up, impromptu, and Phillips moved toward the drawer, far less agilely than he had before. He stooped and took the handle and then hesitated. It was as if the inner workings of his soul were visible in what his body did. He tugged at the handle and pulled out the drawer, then stepped back.

Basil moved toward the corpse hesitantly. He looked at it first in the foreshortened perspective, head to feet, then he went and stood next to the drawer. He stared down at the body. He looked up, bewildered.

"What is Phyllis doing here?"

Part Three

Manfredi

1

For some moments the three men formed a tableau worthy of a Dutch Renaissance painter, their expressions capturing the very meaning of the words astonishment, horror, dread, anger. They traded these emotions among themselves, passing them on, picking them up, the cold thin air of the mortuary basement their perfect carrier.

"Your daughter!"

"Oh my God," cried Phillips.

Basil, never more of a father than when he stood beside the lifeless body of his daughter, her half made-up face contrasting with the shampooed hair and the simple garment covering her nakedness—looked at Manfredi. But the old eyes seemed to pass through the captain to the pages of family albums in which Phyllis, in various stages on the way to this sad end, had figured.

"What happened to her?"

The sight of Phyllis seemed to have driven from his mind the reason for winding down that staircase to this frigid room. It was altogether right and just that Basil's words took substance as he spoke, little articulate puffs, sound made visible.

"It was her body we found in the greenhouse."

"But that was Virginia."

Anger modulated to confusion. This was going to be easier than it had any right to be. He took Basil's arm, to lead him away from the drawer and its awful contents, but Basil shook

235

Manfredi's hand off in a return of anger.

"You made a mistake!"

"A horrible mistake. Gregory thought it was Virginia."

"Impossible. He knows his own sister."

"Professor, there is no satisfactory explanation for what has happened, no adequate excuse. When I brought you down here, I knew only that this was not Virginia. The identification at the house on Collier Avenue was hasty. Not really an identification. An assumption. The hair . . ."

"But you knew her. You had spoken with her."

"I accept full responsibility."

Basil looked at Phillips and then turned away. If he had been capable of such unkindness, his look would have been one of disgust. His estimate of Manfredi was, if possible, lower. He started toward the spiral staircase, waving away all efforts to help him.

"Gregory should be here."

"We have been trying to reach him," Phillips said eagerly.

Basil started slowly up the stairs, boxing the compass as he rose, north, west, south, east, and over again. He paused. "I feel that I should call the police."

The unkindest cut of all. But Manfredi welcomed it. He wanted to be lacerated by criticism, hauled before the board, cashiered, sent at last into retirement but under a cloud. But if Basil, gentle Basil, was stirred to a semblance of indignation, what would the fiery Gregory be?

The best defense is a good offense. Manfredi was willing to be held in contempt by the grieving father, but he was less inclined to be instructed by the son. After all, Gregory had been there, Gregory had made funeral arrangements with Phillips, Gregory had decided that there would be a closed coffin at the wake because of the condition of the corpse.

With that track record, Gregory was certain to fulminate like Torquemada, seeking to dump the complete blame on Manfredi and the police. But it is not the role of the police to identify bodies. Relatives and friends are called in to do that. Manfredi seized upon this as his sole moral underpinning. It was mere accident that he had known the supposed victim and should have seen that the body he himself had unearthed from beneath the floor of the greenhouse was not hers.

But he had fled to the back yard, away from the photographers and other media people who crowded around the sheeted object on the floor of the garage on Collier Avenue. Gregory had been there, next to Sara Sanguinetti. It was more surprising that he had failed to recognize his sister than that Manfredi did not see the body was not Virginia's. This moral tennis match continued in his mind when they had gone upstairs, away from the horrors below.

"You can wait for your son in my office."

"How do I know that he is coming here?"

Manfredi said, "I will go get him."

It was analogous to his leaving the garage on Collier when the body had been laid on the floor. His nerves were going. He no longer felt zest at representing law and order in the chaos of life. Basil looked like a pillow that needed puffing up, the ministrations of a good housemaid. Since he had no idea where he would find Gregory, Manfredi sat in his car in the parking lot and made some calls.

Rachel was rendered dumb by the news, at least for a moment. "How could such a mistake be made?"

"You'll have to ask Gregory."

The outline of his bid for self-respect was now clear. Gregory must bear the brunt of the criticism. Already Manfredi was giving imaginary interviews, explaining the procedure in identifying bodies.

"You dug her up, right?"

"In front of witnesses. The whole thing is taped."

"Who did you think it was?"

"When I had cleared away the dirt, what I was looking at was a sheet."

"With a body in it?"

"That was the surprise. We were there to test Ambrose Hennessy's claim to have buried a body thirty years ago. If I expected to find anything, it was bones."

"Gregory!" Rachel cried.

"He identified the body."

"He doesn't know the difference between Virginia and Phyllis?"

"Rachel, think. This is not a pleasant task for anyone. What does Gregory do all day, talk on the phone, sit at his computer, buy and sell. This is not in his line."

"Tell it to Basil."

"I have."

Rachel wanted to know all about what had just happened at Phillips's. How easily the account was shaped, took on intelligible form, prepared for the surprise as neither he nor Basil had been prepared for the astounding fact that the body in the drawer was not Virginia.

"I am trying to find Gregory."

"Don't ask him to identify anybody."

Alma was not surprised. Nor did she accept Manfredi's extenuation that Gregory's occupation did not equip him for the task he had botched.

"Botching's his middle name. I won't tell you how much money he lost for me."

"Lost?"

"As in paradise. Close to one hundred thousand dollars."

"Ye gods."

"*Di immortales.* You seldom hear that anymore." That easily she was distracted from her financial woes. But Manfredi was surprised.

"I thought he was a financial genius."

"*Caro mio,* investing is like going to the track. There are experts there too, if you care to believe them. I knew what I was doing. 'With my eyes wide open . . .' "

How much money did she have that she could sing away one hundred thousand dollars?

"Have you told Basil yet?"

The story was inevitability already in its second public airing. Manfredi was impressed by the matter of factness of his tone. At one and the same time he conveyed the extraordinary misidentification and the suggestion that these things happen. Basil did not seem to blame Gregory.

"Who does he blame?"

"Your humble servant."

"Whose sister is Phyllis? But don't worry. Basil will see who was at fault."

It was in a far more tolerable mood that Manfredi tried once again to reach Sanguinetti at the morgue. She had been at his side in the greenhouse, she had crouched and lifted the corner of the sheet, exposing the hair and . . . But that is where he himself had turned away. Not before thinking that the woman in the sheet was Virginia, however.

"I think we have the wrong wife."

Had Sanguinetti's pert little remark, worthy of a pathologist in whom all normal sentiments at the sight of death are deeply submerged, been occasioned by anything he himself had said? Had he said, "Virginia?" It would be well for them to review their common experience now, before they had to account for it. The narrative he had tried out on Rachel and Alma was not ready for Broadway until Sara had a shot at any rewrites that might occur to her.

2

At a desk in the lobby, an old man sat erect, sound asleep. Manfredi recognized him. Ray Logelin. They had gone through the academy together. Old man, he had instinctively thought. But Ray was overweight, his hair was cotton white, he looked like Santa in an old Coca-Cola ad. Manfredi went soundlessly past him to the hallway.

"Who's that!"

"Don't shoot, Ray."

"Manfredi!"

How long had it been? Too long. Still on the job? Manfredi had been smart not to retire.

"You think, he's got the pension, any other money he earns is gravy. This is what it comes to, Egidio. Sitting in a goddamn lobby half the night with nothing but stiffs to keep me company."

"You should bring a radio."

"You think this is a hearing aid?" He turned to display the plug in his ear. A cord trailed into his jacket which, when he unzipped it, proved to be attached to a radio. "I'm waiting for the game to start."

"Listen to police radio."

"I can't get it on this." He called after Manfredi when he started down the hallway, "Don't retire."

Why do they need a watchman at the morgue? The strangeness of that seemed to exonerate Ray for sleeping through his watch. Manfredi was in an exonerating mood so far as he and his fellows in the force were concerned.

The light was on in Sara Sanguinetti's office. Manfredi stuck his head in the door. "Hello?"

He went on in when his second hello went unanswered. Her desk chair was halfway across the room and papers were strewn on the floor. Manfredi froze and looked carefully around. A sudden departure? Why? He moved slowly to the windows where the blinds hung awry. There was a severed cord.

Manfredi moved away from the window. His impulse was to call Ray Logelin, but what was the point of that? He left the office and went down the hall to the elevator.

The lab was reached by pressing 1. They might have used zero. Centigrade. The freezing point. He preferred the elevator to those spiral stairs at Phillips. The doors slid open. He had gone tense. What did he expect to see? The room was empty, an operating theater not in use. The lights over the table were on, grisly instruments, the microphone. Coroners gave a running account of what they were doing, taping it for the record, for the enlightenment and amusement of law enforcement officers who might care to catch the performance.

"Hello, hello, hello."

He might have been testing the microphone. It was pretty obvious that the room was empty. But why were the bright lights on over the table? Why had the lights in Sara's office upstairs been on? His eyes were dragged toward the wall with its grim rows of drawers. He moved somnabulantly toward them. One drawer seemed imperfectly shut.

This was a moment of supreme importance. Find out here and now why that drawer was not completely closed or cover his ass. He took out his phone and called the lab.

241

3

He was as much spectator as participant in the drama that followed. A team from the police lab arrived, three men and a girl under the leadership of Popehn who played the harmonica until you wished he would swallow it. It was seldom that these people saw a scene when it was still unclear what it was a scene of.

"The place is empty," Popehn said.

"Not the drawers. Do you notice the one that isn't quite shut?"

He wanted it and everything else dusted for prints. Whatever was going on here, no one was going to say he had acted precipitously. After calling the lab, he had eased the drawer open with the toe of his shoe. He immediately pushed it shut again, not all the way. He used his handkerchief to ease the drawer back to the position that had caught his eye.

His mind was a blank slate on which nothing was written, and he refused to let any letters form on it. Nothing had happened until the whole area was dusted for prints.

"What's with that drawer?"

"Open it."

There is something about a dead body that draws a crowd. Popehn's crew gathered around to look at the lifeless woman looking more lifeless in the morgue lights, then they began to edge away.

"Who is she, Manfredi?"

"Virginia Bauer."

"What did you do, clone her?"

Bodies went headfirst into these drawers and there was a tag on the toe that emerged from the covering. Jane Doe.

"Maybe we ought to check these other drawers."

Gagging sounds from several lab assistants, but Popehn was game. He even did the honors, Manfredi at his side. Little signs of relief when a drawer was empty, a craning to look when it was not. They found her on the fourth try.

"My God, look who it is."

The strangled contorted face of Sara Sanguinetti looked unseeing at a ceiling she perhaps had never looked closely at in life.

"Same way as the other one."

"The other two."

4

Epiphanies come, when they finally do, in bursts. When it rains it pours. Suddenly it was all clear to Manfredi. It seemed fate when he went out to his car and the first thing he got was the call from Noonan.

"I found Gregory Bauer."

"Where is he?"

"He came and took his father home. Phillips is a nervous wreck. Young Bauer is going to sue him and us for everything we have. He is madder than hell. I was glad to see him go."

"He took his father home?"

"Yeah."

"Meet me there."

"Geez."

On the way, Manfredi called Popehn for a preliminary on the comparison of the prints found on the two drawers and those on the blinds in Sanguinetti's office.

"It looks like a match. Whose are they?"

"I'll keep you posted."

An inquiry is defined in terms of results that are not always reached, perhaps only rarely. Ninety-five percent of the time law enforcement personnel are not enforcing the law. Investigations are undertaken in order to provide an answer to a question. The answer is not often found, or if found is productive of other more troubling questions. True as all that was, Manfredi had the certainty that he was about to fulfill his function in an unequivocal way, the questions would be answered and there would be no loose ends. What had baffled him now looked as simple as an exercise in elementary logic.

Cui bono? Who benefits from the death of Virginia? Who benefits from the death of Phyllis? Who is the remaining heir to the fortune Basil Bauer had amassed? What financial wizard has recently fallen upon bad times and expressed envy at what his father had accomplished almost heedlessly, doubtless thinking of such losses as Alma had incurred on expert advice? Who had been a constant presence around Sara Sanguinetti? Sara who had been asked to find some explanation of the body Phillips had in his basement.

A small cloud passed over Manfredi's face. No matter. The thing in its main outlines was clear. He was eager to discuss the matter with the Bauers, father and son.

"How can you show your face here?" Gregory demanded, standing in the doorway, one hand holding the half open door.

"It's hard not to. It's attached to my head."

He walked right into the financial advisor, and they moved back into the room like clumsy dancers.

"What do you think . . ."

"Sit down."

Gregory took up a stance, arms out from his body, feet separated. Manfredi hoped the younger man would try something. On the other hand, there was no need to run risks. He took out his gun.

"I said sit down."

"Is that a gun?" Basil asked, coming into the room. He seemed calm now, as if all the anger had been left to Gregory.

"I find it more convenient than a cord cut from a blind."

Gregory's reaction sufficed to show that the accusation had gone home.

"Why Dr. Sanguinetti, Gregory? There is a stupid logic in killing your sister and Virginia, but Sara?"

Gregory relaxed and sat down. He more or less collapsed in the chair. But then he stirred. "Not Virginia. I didn't do that."

"What are you saying, Gregory?" Basil cried.

Noonan came and had the satisfaction of seeing the hitherto indignant Gregory reduced to a whining son. He kept telling his father that he had not killed Virginia. Basil sat in the middle of a couch, his hands pressed flat on the other cushions, keening and waiting for his friends to arrive.

It was one of the anomalies of the case that Gregory continued to insist that he had not killed Virginia. One might have thought that he would have denied killing his sister. His story was that having killed Phyllis and buried her in the greenhouse on Collier, where the two of them had grown up, inspired by the story Ambrose Hennessy was telling, he then began to notice a strange smell in the car he had rented. His story about arriving by plane was thus discarded. He had rented the car in Chicago and arrived in Fort Elbow on the Thursday. He had had it for days when he looked in the trunk and found the body of Virginia. She had been strangled in the same way he had strangled his sister. He thought he was going mad. Had he killed her and put her in the trunk and forgotten it? How long had she been there? He took another sheet from the linen closet at his father's apartment, intending to bury Virginia where she would never be found. But then conversations with Sara Sanguinetti suggested another way. He drove up to the delivery entrance of the morgue, carried Virginia inside, slipped her into a drawer, attaching the Jane Doe tag to her toe.

He demanded that they inspect the rental car. He had run it through a car wash several times, and had them perfume the trunk as well as the interior, but he could still smell that dreadful smell.

The resources of the police department did not permit checking out this fantastic story. One way or the other, it did not alter the fate of Gregory Bauer. Besides, they would then have to ask who had put the dead body of Virginia in the trunk of Gregory's car. On the whole it was much simpler to assume that Gregory had.

Q.E.D.

Ambrose

1

"Better a believable impossibility than an unbelievable possibility, as Aristotle said."

"Why does he insist on it? Even if true . . ."

"*Non e vero, ma e ben trovato.* Or, conversely, *non e falso ma e mal trovato.*"

Alma had made several attempts at reconstructing events as Gregory recounted them, but the pons asinorum remained the claim that someone had left the dead body of Virginia in the trunk of his rented car and that, skipping a few details, he had dropped her off at the morgue, sliding her into one of drawers designed for cadavers.

"That sounds like a kind of underwear."

"Now, Alma."

The great Seymour had taken on Gregory as a client, and Basil was reconciled to severe punishment but nothing that would endanger his son's life. "Thank God there's no death penalty."

"Oh?"

"Seymour tells me he is unlikely even to get a life sentence."

"We all get that, Basil. But Seymour is doubtless right. By the time Gregory is your age he will be out on the streets again."

"I am seventy-two years old!"

"Of course I am taking good behavior into account."

Circumstances unimaginable when we are not in them

dictate possibilities when we are. The media were calling Gregory a serial murderer. There was no overlooking the fact that he had been guilty of sororicide in the case of Phyllis and treachery in the case of Sara Sanguinetti. She had believed his interest in her was genuine and personal. How had he managed to do her in?

"I was illustrating to her how I thought Virginia had been killed. It was the method I had copied with Phyllis. I cut a length from the blind cord, moved theatrically behind her chair and then went to work. When she realized what was happening, she struggled."

"You intended to kill her?"

"I had no choice. She had been telling me the contents of the report she would make to the lab. I counted on Phillips to hush up his mistake and bury Phyllis as Virginia. I had already deposited Virginia in a drawer downstairs. I cannot tell you how alarmed I was when I located the source of the odd smell in my rented car."

And he was off again on the story that no one would credit, that the body of Virginia had been put in his trunk by somebody else. If Gregory were not so guilty, Ambrose would have felt more so.

"Suggesting of course that there is another homicidal maniac running loose," as he spelled it out later for Basil.

"Ambrose, you should talk to him. Urge him to make a clean breast of it."

"Father Jim has been to see him."

"That ought to help."

"He believes Gregory."

"Why strain at a gnat? He believes his services are boffo box office with the students."

" 'When a man stops believing in God he will believe anything.' Chesterton."

Ambrose did, however, visit Gregory.

2

"I had hoped to visit you in your cell." They had brought Gregory into a room where inmates consulted their lawyers.

"You wouldn't if you had to be there."

"But you forget, Gregory, I preceded you here. They actually locked me up, as the result of your badgering the police to do something."

"Why did you say you killed my mother?"

"Because I did."

"Come on."

Ambrose smiled. Truth was always the best disguise. He had sequestered the notebook that led up to the great event.

31.x—Witticisms in their season delight but how I loathe it now when he moons about Nectar and Ambrosia. I told him he has the genders wrong, but he counters by saying that Greek loan words are masculine in Italian. How I long to hear his last last word.

1.xi—Lugubrious on the feast of all souls...it is the name of an Oxford college as well. A says he said a rosary for the most neglected soul in purgatory. While trying to get his hand up my skirt. To think that once his boldness excited me. He told me a story of killing a girl once, a kitchen helper at Dowling Hall. I can ask Basil if I don't believe him. So watch out.

3.xi—Basil says it's nonsense. A girl drowned and Ambrose imagined that he'd had a love affair with her. He had told her that they would never see one another again after Ambrose graduated. The next morning she was found floating in the lake.

★ ★ ★ ★ ★

Couldn't have such entries attracting attention now. How boring it was to plow through the endless pages of those notebooks in which Lilian had proved daily how rare a well-turned phrase is. In the end, he gained custody of them all.

"Poor Virginia had hardly gotten started on her project." Basil cast a sad look at the stacks of Lilian's notebooks.

"I'll take over," Ambrose said.

"Would you?"

"It would give me enormous pleasure to edit them, Basil."

"When I was held in a cell here," Ambrose continued to Gregory, "it was my overpowering feeling that I belonged there. That it was my destiny. You must develop a similar attitude. It will be your exclusive setting for the foreseeable future."

"My God, you're encouraging."

"Jean Paul Sartre held that our freedom is absolute. 'But what of the man in prison,' he was asked. 'Is he still free? *Mais bien sur.* He is as free as you and I. But he is locked up behind bars. And what are they? They restrict his freedom. Only if he wills it. It is only if he desires to be elsewhere that the bars can confine and restrict him. They are, consequently, the result of his freedom, not its denial.' "

"Was he ever in jail?"

"They could never prove anything."

"Why did you feel you belonged here?"

"For the same reason you do."

Gregory had taken up smoking, perhaps in the hope of shortening his life. He had a way of blowing smoke at his visitor.

"Who do you think put Virginia's body in the trunk of my car?"

"I did."

"Ambrose, I am serious."

"You must demand that the police pursue the matter."

"They laugh at me."

"What does Seymour say?"

"We have enough trouble without complicating matters with a story like that. He doesn't believe me."

"I believe you, Gregory." And Ambrose patted the lad on the arm.

"God bless you, Ambrose."

3

"It is so good of you to go see him, Ambrose."

Basil could have been forgiven if he had reacted like Job to his travails. He had had children. Now he had none. He had had wives. Now he had none. These losses had the perverse effect of making Basil seem youthful. He had completed the move back to the Residenza and this gave him a new lease on life as well as on his old rooms.

"It is not good for man to live alone."

"I hope you are not planning to marry again, Basil."

"God forbid. I am a mortal danger to any wife of mine."

"You mustn't blame yourself."

"I don't."

Basil's conscience was obviously as clear as his eyes. But he had a way now of speaking too softly for Ambrose's new hearing aids to pick up his voice easily. Ambrose had a printed sign saying Louder!, which he took from his pocket like a soccer ref all too often when talking with Basil.

"You should not have told Alma that I made up the story about Maureen."

"I said you dramatized it."

"I killed her."

"She fell off the dock."

"You didn't see me push her?"

"You didn't push her."

"Basil, I need not tell you that one can act by not acting as well as acting."

"That is paradoxical."

"Life is paradoxical."

But the etymology of the world related to language, incompatible statements. Was the world made up of statements? Some mad philosophers have thought so. But the world of statements is the world of statements.

"Our world, Basil."

"Man is the animal who talks."

"I meant particularly our world."

No need to spell it out for Basil, his oldest friend. *Magis amicus veritas?* Not on your life. Their friendship rather than truth. Or rather the special truth that was their friendship.

"Last night as I lay in bed I thought of Dowling Hall, and I walked in imagination down the corridor from study hall to chapel. Under those hanging lamps shaped like bombs, suspended in wrought iron fixtures, and on my left the closed doors of classrooms, on my right the darkened windows that look out on the courtyard. To the end where the intersecting hall leads on the left to the glass doors of the auditorium and to the right extends the whole width of the school to far off glass windows. Slowly now. If it were day I could walk along the loggia that is parallel to this inner corridor, re-entering at a point just before the doors of the refectory are reached. When one comes in from the loggia there, he sees the staircase that leads up to the faculty corridor on the second floor and the sophomore dormitory on the third. But I continue down the hallway, more classrooms to my right, windows looking out over the loggia to the left. The rector's office and then that stairway. And, and. . . ."

Ambrose looked at Basil, who nodded. Yes, that is how it was.

How it is, how it is.

Yes, of course.

There were tears in Ambrose's eyes, the sentimental tears of a man aged into his eighth decade whose past was more vivid to him than any present, forget about the future. The dull plane of the world receded and he bade it adieu without compunction. Left behind were all the tedious distinctions between good and evil, the intended and happenstance, the forced and free. Gone too the distinction between the quick and the dead. In memory, in imagination, Lilian was as alive as Basil. As Virginia and Alma too, and dear pie-faced Maureen, her body lifting gently with the waters of the lake, had an equal claim on their attention.

"Ambrose."

"Basil."

"What did you expect them to find when they tore up the floor of the greenhouse?"

"The bricks were carefully removed, Basil, one at a time."

"They should be replaced."

"We could make it a project."

"I would like that. There is no material like bricks to give one a sense of having accomplished something."

"Then we two will we do it."

"Now answer my question."

"You will have to repeat it."

"What did you think they would find beneath the floor of the greenhouse?"

"Lilian."

Basil laughed melodiously. "You are terrible, Ambrose. Incorrigible."

"They didn't dig deep enough."

Below the level of the bricks, already below ground level, beneath the few feet that Manfredi had dug, beneath the present and the here and now, down, down, through the contemporaneous levels of time and memory where forever he pursues and she pursued, down to the ultimate stratum.

"And what is that?"

"Dowling Hall."

Two old men in a retirement home, their sins and flaws too familiar to elicit remorse, the line between what they had done and what they thought they had done blurred beyond all repair, nodding in agreement with what the other had not said.

"I murdered Maureen."

"I did not like my children."

"My memories of Lilian begin to fade, yet I can still hear the first poem of hers I ever read. I asked her to recite it for me, and she did, beautifully, yet when I remember it I hear my own voice."

If Iris is the apple of his eye
What discord could he possibly descry
Between a girl he held and a girl beheld
That could not right off be repelled?

4

Some months later, after winter had come and gone, and it was spring again, Marian Casey told Ambrose over a glass of Sardinian red and a stolen cigarette of the troubles the new owner was having with the house on Collier Avenue.

"Their solution was to have the greenhouse removed and with it all allusions to you know what."

"Not unwise of them, I should say."

"No, you shouldn't. They are having no end of trouble with our Indian friends."

"You don't say."

"Would you believe that they came upon some bones and the contractor stopped work immediately. He has some fraction of Native American blood. The chief has his back up. He wants the city to declare the place a burial ground and deed it back to its rightful owners."

"And make no bones about it?"

"And of course they are suing me."

"Poor Marian."

"Is that all you can say? Don't you have some brilliant scheme for me?"

"Of course. Have those bones tested to see if they are indeed Native American."

"Not on your life. Can you imagine the uproar?"

"You're probably right."

"I have this eerie waking dream that those bones are going to rise up and clatter around the premises."

"And point an accusing finger?"

Marian sipped as she should the lovely wine. Ambrose began to tell her of a wonderful three days he had spent in Sassari where he first came to know this wine. Actually it was on the boat from Civitavecchia. But her mind was still on bones.

"These bones will live again," she murmured. "What's that text from the Bible, Ambrose? You would know."

"Oh, this is no time for Ezechial." He reached over and patted her leg, the bone plushly padded in flesh. Two sinners in this vale of tears, he far more than she.

"Enjoy your wine."

NORMAL PUBLIC LIBRARY
NORMAL, ILLINOIS 61761